Cherry Blossom Baseball

In the same series

When the Cherry Blossoms Fell

Cherry Blossom Winter

Also by Jennifer Maruno

Warbird

Totem

Kid Soldier

Cherry Blossom Baseball

A Cherry Blossom Book

Jennifer Maruno

DUNDURN
TORONTO

Editor: Allister Thompson
Design: Laura Boyle
Composite image and cover design: Laura Boyle
Cover images: © KPG_Payless/shutterstock.com (girl); Blossom image © Elizabeth Bernstein/Dreamstime.com
Printer: Webcom

Library and Archives Canada Cataloguing in Publication

Maruno, Jennifer 1950-, author
Cherry blossom baseball : a cherry blossom book / Jennifer Maruno., author

Issued in print and electronic formats.

ISBN 978-1-4597-3166-0 (pbk.).--ISBN 978-1-4597-3167-7 (pdf).--
ISBN 978-1-4597-3168-4 (epub)

1. Japanese Canadians--Evacuation and relocation, 1942-1945--Juvenile fiction.
I. Title.

PS8626.A785C537 2015 jC813'.6 C2015-902195-2
C2015-902196-0

1 2 3 4 5 19 18 17 16 15

We acknowledge the support of the **Canada Council for the Arts** and the **Ontario Arts Council** for our publishing program. We also acknowledge the financial support of the **Government of Canada** through the **Canada Book Fund** and **Livres Canada Books**, and the **Government of Ontario** through the **Ontario Book Publishing Tax Credit** and the **Ontario Media Development Corporation**.

Printed and bound in Canada.

Visit us at

Dundurn.com | @dundurnpress | Facebook.com/dundurnpress | Pinterest.com/dundurnpress

Dundurn
3 Church Street, Suite 500
Toronto, Ontario, Canada
M5E 1M2

For Ruby Jane

Chapter 1

AUGUST 1944

Michiko had been making tea for her mother and her aunt for so long, she could do it in her sleep. She filled the chipped enamel kettle, placed it on the electric element, and turned the knob. Then she pulled the metal caddy from the shelf, removed the lid, and scooped *cha* into the blue porcelain pot. *Half gone*, she thought with a smile as she looked at what was left in the caddy. The lower the level of bits of green leaves and tiny twigs, the closer they were to leaving the apartment above the drugstore.

"We already gave this place a spring cleaning," Sadie said, entering the kitchen. "Your mother is far too fussy." Michiko's aunt removed the coloured kerchief tied around her head and gave her shiny, straight, black hair a toss. Her nail polish, lipstick, perfume, and earrings made her, in Michiko's eyes, the most modern woman in the world.

Michiko nodded as she placed the little blue cups with no handles on the table. It wouldn't be long before the cups would be packed with the other dishes in the wooden cartons stacked next to the sink. When Michiko had suggested they make tea in the cups and pack the pot, her mother had frowned. "Tea made in a cup does not have the same taste as from a pot," she'd said. "The teapot will be the very last thing to be wrapped."

The whistle of the kettle brought Michiko's mother, Eiko, into the kitchen.

"I'm parched," she said as she slumped into the wooden chair. "I'd better stop, it's almost time for the baby to wake."

Michiko poured each of them a steaming cup of pale green liquid. "There really aren't a lot of things to take," she said.

"When I think of all we could have brought when we first came to this ghost of a town …" Sadie said in a quiet, sad voice. "You had curtains, carpets, and bedspreads. There were pictures on the wall, china, and silverware." She put her head in her hands. Her razor-sharp hair fell across her cheek. "And I had a closet full of clothes and a whole tower of hat boxes."

"Stop it," Eiko said, putting down her cup. "What are a few hats and dresses compared with meeting the man of your dreams?" Her oval face and almond-shaped eyes were almost an exact copy of Sadie's, only more serious. "Always remember, 'Every reverse side has its reverse side.'"

"You sound just like Geechan," Michiko said as she sat down.

"I know," her mother said. "His old sayings fill my head these days."

"Odd you would say that," Sadie said. "Sometimes I think I can hear his voice."

"Sometimes," Michiko said with a sigh, "I hear him in the garden." She looked toward the back window, remembering her beloved grandfather patting down plants with long, thin fingers. His face and hands were always brown, with lots of wrinkles, just like a chestnut. When he wasn't hoeing or weeding, he was out walking. Every day he took a new route, smiling at neighbours, talking to dogs and children, always on the lookout for the right-sized rock for his garden's pathway. He had even spelled out the word WELCOME in small white stones across the flowerbed in front of the store. There was talk his garden could be on a postcard.

"Look what I found," Eiko said as she drew a small packet of blue envelopes and paper from her apron pocket and put it on the table. "They were taped to the back of the bureau."

Michiko undid the string that tied them together and lifted the tattered sheaves of passport papers from the top. She unfolded them to see the photograph of a young man in a dark peaked cap and high-collared jacket. "How old was he in this picture?"

"Sixteen," both women said at the same time.

"Only five years older than me?" Michiko sat back in amazement. "He was so young."

"He came to Canada, like so many others, to make his fortune," Sadie said. She took a small sip of tea. "Everyone in Japan told stories about the land where gold washed down the river."

"And Geechan was going to return with a suitcase full of it," Michiko said, repeating the tale she had heard her grandfather tell so many times before.

"He was very proud of his passport," her mother said. "It was the kind that allowed him to stay in Canada." She pulled a small, worn card from the pile.

"What's that?" Michiko asked, taking it from her mother's hand. "*Inspection Card*," she read out loud, "*Yokohama, Japan, May, 1923*. That's funny."

"What's funny?"

Michiko ran her finger across the numbers along the bottom. "They stamped it but forgot to circle the number of his cabin."

"That's because he didn't have a cabin," Sadie said. "He travelled steerage. All he got was a bunk in the hull of the ship."

Michiko pulled one of the thin, almost transparent sheets of blue paper from its envelope and examined the rows of elegant black characters. "What do they say?"

"Just a lot of old news from old friends," her mother responded with a sigh. "Stories of people who died, people who married, and babies born."

Michiko slid the paper back into the envelope and turned it over. "It looks like an address on the back," she said. "Maybe we should write to tell them that Geechan has ..." She stopped, unable to bring herself to say, "died."

"There is no guarantee anyone would still be at the same address," her mother said, straightening the small stack. "These were sent long ago, before the war."

"And," Sadie said, "mailing letters to Japan will only

arouse suspicion." She raised her teacup to her sister for more tea and added. "Don't forget why we are all here in the first place."

"Because we are all spies," Michiko said in a flat, disinterested voice. She put the card back on the pile of papers.

Sadie turned to Michiko. "Do you remember Geechan's toilet story?"

Michiko couldn't help but smile as she remembered her grandfather telling them that they did not have toilets in Japan like the ones in Canada, and he had almost washed his face in the large white porcelain bowl when he first came to Vancouver.

"Remember he wanted us to bow to his picture of the emperor whenever we passed it?" Sadie asked Eiko with a grin.

"That was the day you told him the emperor had a funny nose," Eiko said. "He was not happy about that."

Michiko recalled the picture of Emperor Hirohito that hung in her grandparents' apartment in the tall wooden building on Powell Street. But her grandfather's house and their own brick bungalow on the other side of Vancouver were just faded memories. "Geechan never asked me to bow to the emperor's picture," she said, turning the envelope toward her.

"That's because you were Canadian-born," her mother said.

"But you were born in Canada too," Michiko said. "Why did he want you to bow?"

"It doesn't matter now," her mother said in an exasperated tone that signalled the end of the talk. She gathered up the passport and letters and put them back in the pocket of her apron.

Michiko thought about the imposing emperor standing as stiff as a scarecrow in his embroidered robes and enormously thick wooden shoes. Shoes had been on her mind a lot these days. The straps of the black patents she'd worn for her aunt's wedding already pinched her ankles. Her father had punched a new hole in the tip of the thin, pointed straps, but there was no room for another. She was so tired of polishing over the scuffs on the white leather saddle of her shoes. Michiko was desperate for a pair of running shoes, but her mother told her that not only did they not give enough support, they also looked shabby.

"Your clothes don't have to be expensive, but they do have to be presentable," her mother said, time and time again. "They tell the world who you are." She still shook her head with disapproval when she talked about the family whose children had worn dirty canvas shoes to the Sato wedding. Ever since then she'd had a strong dislike of runners.

Even so, Michiko wrote down the page number and their cost on a piece of paper and attached it to the front of the catalogue, just in case her mother changed her mind. In weeks, Michiko hoped she would be slipping her feet into brand new running shoes, ready to race from first base to home plate in seconds.

"Yoo-hoo," a familiar voice hollered from the bottom of the back stairwell. Mrs. Morrison, their longtime friend, called up to them. "Are you ready?"

"Coming," Sadie called back. She turned to her sister

with concern. "Why don't we wait for the baby to wake up?" she whispered. "It's a perfect day for a walk."

Michiko knew there was no point in expecting her mother to visit Geechan's grave. She hadn't visited it since he passed away. Every night, as Eiko prepared dinner, tears rolled down her cheeks in long, silent lines. Her mother pretended it was the onions, but Michiko knew it wasn't. Like all the Japanese people in this poor, abandoned town, her mother tried to make their problems invisible by hiding her feelings.

"I have to feed her," Eiko said. "You go ahead."

Sadie took a few minutes to wrap a rice ball in a piece of wax paper.

Michiko grabbed the red baseball cap with the large white "A" from the hook at the top of the stairs and shoved it on her head. It used to belong to her Uncle Kaz when he played for the Asahi team, but he had given it to her as a birthday present. It was a bit large, but she didn't care. She raced down the stairs to join the woman who waited in their back vestibule.

Mrs. Morrison's big, red, freckled arms clutched a bunch of daisies. Her wide-brimmed straw hat and floral dress with its puffy skirt made her look like one enormous bouquet. Her thick beige stockings made Michiko smile, thinking of her aunt's earlier story.

"Instead of stockings," Sadie had explained, "the movie stars wear liquid makeup." Then she leaned back in her chair and lifted her bare leg in the air to demonstrate the application of a Helena Rubinstein leg stick. "It gives your leg a smooth, stocking-like sheen."

Michiko had covered her mouth with her hands and giggled. And they'd laughed out loud when Sadie lost her balance and ended up on the floor.

"You're looking very happy this morning," Mrs. Morrison said, seeing the wide smile on Michiko's face.

"I was thinking about new shoes," Michiko said.

Mrs. Morrison looked down at her own worn ones. "Suppose I should think about a new pair as well, but these are just so darn comfortable, I hate to give them up."

She pulled three of the flowers away from the bouquet and handed them to Michiko. "Take these upstairs for your mother," she said. "She likes to arrange a … you know, what she calls her vase for your grandfather."

"A *tokonoma*," Michiko said, supplying the Japanese word. "She will like that."

Michiko knew her mother would use her special pair of short, sharp scissors to trim the stems. Then she would wind them with thin wire to keep the flowers straight and tall before placing them into the small cluster of pins that rested in the well of the square ceramic tray.

At the cemetery, Michiko picked up the pickle jar they used for a flower vase on her grandfather's grave. She removed the dead flowers and dumped the sour, murky water over the roots of the small cherry tree behind the gravestone. Then she carried the jar to the metal tap that stuck up out of the ground. Michiko remembered how angry Sadie had become when she'd found out there was running water for the cemetery, but not for the little huts where the Japanese people lived. But that had changed. All the wooden houses had water and electricity now.

"I wonder if Geechan can see the flowers we bring?" Michiko said.

"I think so," Sadie said. "I think he can smell and hear, too. He just can't taste and touch," she said as she placed the small rice ball on the cement stone.

"So why did you bring food?"

"So he can smell it," Sadie said. "The smell of good food always made him happy."

Michiko couldn't argue with that. Her grandfather had loved to eat, even though he was always as thin as a rake.

Sadie took the fresh flowers from Mrs. Morrison and spread them on the ground. One by one, she arranged them in the jar.

They all paused for a moment at the gateway of the small stone wall that surrounded the cemetery. "He should have been buried with our mother," Sadie murmured. "It isn't right to be so far away from her."

Mrs. Morrison put her hand on top of Sadie's and patted it.

"Will you visit him when we're gone?" Michiko asked.

"Of course," Mrs. Morrison said. She pulled a handkerchief from beneath the cuff of her sleeve and wiped a tear from her eye. "When you write to me, I will come here and read him every one of your letters."

Chapter 2

GOODBYE GIFTS

A fist rapped at window of the drugstore. "Hi, Clarence," Michiko called out as she unlocked the front door. The small bell overhead jangled when the tall, lanky boy, with a nose covered with freckles and eyelashes that were almost invisible, stepped inside. Tufts of golden hair stuck out from his grass-stained baseball cap.

"I thought I'd drop this off," he said, handing her a brown paper bag.

Michiko removed a flat, hinged box, painted sky blue. A tiny gold clasp held it shut.

"It's just a cigar box," Clarence said with a shrug. "I figured it's good for keeping stuff."

Michiko ran her hand across the lid. It was as smooth as glass.

"After I sanded it, I remembered what your father told me about straining the paint first," he said with a grin. "I used one of my sister's socks."

Her father and Clarence got along well. Whenever they met, Sam gave Clarence a soft cuff on the cheek. Clarence would duck away and then put up his fists. After a few harmless jabs, her father ruffled the boy's already unruly hair.

"Thanks," Michiko said, lowering her eyes. "I'm making you something too, but it isn't quite finished." She began to worry about his goodbye gift. A bouquet of origami flowers seemed a good idea at the time, but now she wasn't quite sure.

"No problem," Clarence said, sticking his hands into his back pockets. "You won't be leaving for a while. I just thought I'd better get this to you before one of my sisters wanted it."

Michiko's eyes widened. Now she knew the flowers were a mistake. The moment he took them home, they would tease him. She would have to think of something else.

"How about a few pitches?" Clarence asked.

Michiko nodded. She ran up the stairs and pulled her baseball cap from its peg. "I won't be long," she yelled through the open apartment door.

Clarence walked with his catcher's mitt dangling from the end of the bat over his shoulder. "George is going to meet us at the field," he said.

"Are you still trying to teach George how to pitch?" Michiko asked.

"I told him to practise skipping stones to work on his arm," Clarence said with a grin. "That guy doesn't know how to do anything."

George King knows how to make trouble, Michiko thought. *From the day we arrived he made sure I knew Japs weren't welcome in his town.* She grabbed Clarence's arm. "Do you think George told anyone about my uncle's boat?" she asked. "He promised not to say anything."

Clarence's eyes narrowed. He curled back his lips and sucked through his teeth. "If he did, he'll have me to deal with," he said, clenching his fist, "and he knows it."

It was a short walk down the street to the abandoned lot that had become the town's baseball field. The afternoon sun reddened the bare earth diamond. Clarence removed his glove and handed Michiko the bat. "Let's practise our bunts."

Michiko knew bunting was so much more than just a short hit. Her Uncle Kaz had taught both of them how to land the ball halfway down the third baseline to make the throw to first base a long one. She knew exactly which way to turn her body and how to hold the bat. She was good at bunting and was proud of it.

She stood at the rice bag stuffed with straw they used for home plate, gripping the worn bat handle. Clarence drew back his arm. He snapped it forward, and the ball came towards her. She changed the grip on her bat and bunted the ball right to the third base line. Clarence picked it up just as George King arrived.

George reached into the carrier basket of his bike and removed his catcher's mitt. Michiko couldn't help admiring his new black canvas shoes with their clean white toes.

She leaned against the bat, thinking about her Uncle Ted. The first boat he ever made was for a *hakujin.* When they took it out for a test, he wrote her family to say it sliced through the water like a *sashimi* knife. Michiko had drawn a picture of the ten men it took to help him launch it down the rails and mailed it to him.

Ted's reputation as a boat builder grew beyond his small garage and got him work as a designer in the Atagi shipyard near Vancouver. But after the Japanese bombed Pearl Harbor and the United States joined the war against Japan, the Canadian government seized all the boats that belonged to the Japanese and towed them away. Ted lost his boat, his job, and his pay. He told Michiko later, when they moved to the ghost town, that the ten men in her picture were all put in road camps to work on the railway, just like her father.

In the ghost town, Ted was put in charge of building the houses in the orchard. The government had told him to burn the leftover lumber, but Ted was not one to waste. He built a little rowboat and launched it on Carpenter Creek, behind the old apple depository. As her family watched it bob on the water, their hearts soared with hope. Not hopes of escape, or of spying, but of fresh fish for dinner, sunny days on the lake, and swimming adventures.

But any thoughts of her uncle's little red boat worried Michiko to no end. Last week, having dropped off her mother's quilt square at the church hall, she heard Mrs. Morrison talking to someone on the church's front step.

Michiko recognized George's mother's voice and hid behind the snowball bush to watch and wait for her to leave. She didn't like this tall woman with her cold, superior smile.

"I am only doing my patriotic duty," Mrs. King had said in her sharp, shrill voice. "I take no pleasure in informing the authorities."

"What is it now?" Mrs. Morrison responded wearily.

Michiko saw Mrs. King look around the street and then lean in to speak. "I have reason to believe one of those Japanese men has a boat."

"What makes you think that?" Mrs. Morrison asked. "And where would he keep it?"

"Hidden, of course," Mrs. King said with a wave of her hand. "The point is it is against the law for anyone of Japanese origin to own a boat."

"Let me ask you something," Mrs. Morrison said, puffing up like a courting dove. "Was your husband born in this country?"

"Of course he was," Mrs. King answered in a clipped voice. "Robert grew up down the street from us. What a silly question."

"Would it be all right if he owned a boat?"

"Of course it would be all right if he owned a boat. But he doesn't." Mrs. King waved her hands about her face as if she was shooing flies. "I'm not talking about Mr. King owning a boat, although we certainly could afford one."

Mrs. Morrison gave a large sigh. "My husband was born in this country as well," she said. "Is it all right if he owns a boat?"

"Edna," Mrs. King said with exasperation, "Ralph knows so much about boats, he is in the navy. You are being ridiculous."

"You are the one being ridiculous," Mrs. Morrison said, placing her hands on her ample hips. "Almost all of the Japanese here were born in Canada. Who cares if they own a boat?"

"The government cares," Mrs. King said, clenching her fists. "They could be spying."

"In this unimportant town?" Mrs. Morrison asked. Then she paused, put her finger to her chin, and frowned. "Unless," she said, "unless someone has reason to be watching someone who comes and goes a lot. Like your husband, for example. He does an awful lot of travelling for a small-town banker." Edna rubbed her hands together. "You know, maybe you *should* report your suspicious boat. The authorities could find out if your husband is being watched. Who knows what it might all reveal."

Mrs. King's face went ashen. "I don't know why you have to drag my husband into this."

"I'm not dragging anyone into anything," Mrs. Morrison replied. "You're the one dragging the lake for spies."

Michiko crept out from behind the bush into the sunlight to see Mrs. King marching off in one direction as Mrs. Morrison strolled away in the other. She blew a kiss after Mrs. Morrison.

"Just three people?" George asked in his usual whiny voice, bringing her back to the baseball diamond. "How can we play a game of baseball with just three people, especially when one is a girl?"

"We're not having a game," Clarence answered with exasperation. "I told you we would be having a practice." He turned back to Michiko.

She positioned herself over the plate, determined to hit the ball. This time she tapped it with the tip of the bat. It bounced foul.

"You dipped your shoulder," said a deep voice from behind. She peered out from under her oversized cap and smiled. Her Uncle Kaz picked up the ball and walked over to Clarence.

"How's her pitching?" he asked.

"A lot better than her hitting," Clarence said with a grin. "She's got a good swing, but she's afraid of the ball."

"I am not," Michiko yelled back, even though she knew Clarence was right.

"You playing tonight?" Clarence asked Kaz as he left them to their practice.

"Behind the Bachelors' House," Kaz said. "You coming to watch?"

Michiko smiled. Kaz was talking about the house she'd lived in when they'd first arrived in town, ahead of the other Japanese people. When her family moved to the apartment over the drugstore, Michiko's uncle had filled the bedrooms with bunks for single men. The empty apple depository behind it had become the headquarters for the Men's Baseball Team. All summer long, under the watchful eye of the RCMP, they had been allowed to travel to other camps for tournaments, and they were in the lead.

"Stop closing your eyes and keep them on the ball," Clarence said. "How can you be such a great pitcher but such a terrible hitter?"

I'm not closing my eyes, Michiko thought, *I'm just blinking hard.* She repositioned herself, determined to make a hit.

Clarence pitched again. This time Michiko slammed a hard grounder.

George watched it roll past him.

"That thing in your hand is called a mitt," Clarence yelled at him.

George ran after the ball, picked it up, and walked to the plate. "My turn at bat," he said, grabbing it out of her hand. "Where did you get this bat, anyway? It looks stolen."

Michiko handed him the bat and went into the field. In a short while, her family would be out of this town for good. She couldn't wait to get away from all these suspicions and bad feelings.

Chapter 3

FINAL PLANS

"I want you to sit down with me sometime this week to help me with a budget," Michiko's mother said to Sadie as she took some potatoes from the burlap bag under the sink.

"We can do it now if you want," Sadie said. She sat flipping through a stack of *Hollywood Star* magazines she had taken from the drugstore rack. "No need for me to hurry home; Kaz won't be back for a few days."

"Where has he gone?" Michiko asked, putting her little brother Hiro into his highchair. At one time not very long ago, no one could leave the camp. Now that the rules had changed, people were flying off in all directions looking for work, but not to the other side of the mountains, toward the coast.

"A meeting, Miss Nosy," Sadie said.

"What kind of meeting?" Michiko asked, but no sooner had the words flown out of her mouth than she knew she would be reprimanded for being rude. "I'm sorry," she said as her mother turned to give her a cold stare.

Eiko dried her hands on her apron. She handed Hiro a small piece of raw potato as she came to the table. "Is it to do with you-know-what?"

Sadie nodded.

How Michiko hated those three little words. Every time she heard them, it meant they had discussed something that she was not to know about. If she asked, she was rude. If she eavesdropped, she was *yancha*. How was she ever supposed to know out what was going on in her own family?

"Things will be fine," Eiko said as she patted her sister's hand. "They won't take him."

Michiko frowned. *That's the first time I've ever heard anyone hope that someone wouldn't get a job. What kind of job can it be?*

"Things can't get any worse," Sadie said. "We will both be out of work once they shut the camp and close the schools for good."

"Why doesn't he just work at the drugstore?" Michiko said. "He could take Dad's place."

"Because, Little Miss Fix-it," her aunt said, "Kaz's college education would be wasted in this ghost town." She put her hands to her head. "Our mother moved from a bamboo hut to a cold water flat to living quarters above her own shop. I've gone from my own apartment to a rented hotel room. I should have a house by now."

"Which is exactly why I am making a budget," Eiko said. "I plan to save every penny I can for a home. Sam is going to make fifty-one dollars a week. We have no rent to pay. I figure twenty dollars for food and thirty for everything else. The salary I make as housekeeper at the new place can go into the bank. It will be a crunch, but worth it. What do you think?"

Michiko heard her father's footsteps on the stairs just as the delivery truck out front started up. He came into the kitchen holding a brown paper bag. "Did I hear the word 'crunch'?" He held up the bag and shook it. "Guess what I've got?"

"Did the peanut man come?" Michiko asked, leaping from her chair. Her father had said at breakfast that a man was coming by to fill the vending machine that had come by freight last week. Michiko loved the little red machine with the glass hopper. After putting in a penny, you were to put one hand under the chute, turn the crank with the other, and peanuts were supposed to fall into your hand. She couldn't wait to taste them.

"He did," Sam said, shaking the bag for all to hear. He poured a few of the small red-skinned nuts into each person's hand.

Hiro lifted his hand to his mouth, pushed in the whole batch, and crunched them with enthusiasm. Then he wiped his fingers on the front of his shirt and stuck out his hand for more.

Sadie, who only ate one or two of anything, poked them about with her finger first, selecting the best. After examining it, she placed it in her mouth, and gave the rest to Hiro.

Michiko popped them in two at a time but sucked them before she crunched. She wanted to make the taste last forever. With all this talk of a budget, she knew there would be no spare pennies for peanuts.

Sam gave his clasped fist a shake to move a few nuts between his fingers and thumb, then into his mouth. Shake and pop, shake and pop, then he dusted his fingers to remove the salt. "Ted stopped by," he told them. "He's going to miss Sunday dinner because the lumber company is sending him north again. In fact, he might not be back before we leave."

"We have to see him before we leave," Michiko said. She was desperate to warn him about Mrs. King's suspicions. "I want to tell him something."

"He's going to telephone us on Sunday," her father called out behind him as he headed back down the stairs. Even though the shop closed at noon on Wednesdays, he still worked to keep the store in tip-top condition.

Michiko kept forgetting about the newly installed telephone with its very important party line, the RCMP office down the street. The doctor used it to call through prescriptions, and the hospital left messages for people in town.

Michiko gathered the stack of magazines from the table into her arms and followed her father down the stairs. *If I am Miss Nosy and Miss Fix-it,* she thought, *Aunt Sadie is Mrs. Help-Yourself. No one lets me take magazines from the store.* After placing them back on the rack, Michiko realized it was time to get the mail, one of the jobs her parents had given her but not one she particularly enjoyed.

The post office was at the front of the general store down the street. Groceries were on one side and dry goods at the back. The mail counter had a tiny wicket with slots for letters behind it. The postmistress, the widow of a local farmer, stood behind it in her usual white-collared black dress. Her face had a look that might be a smile, but Michiko knew it was a sneer. The woman's prejudice was as powerful as ammonia. You could smell it even before she spoke.

"Too early," the woman said as soon as Michiko approached the wicket. Her voice was full of bitterness. "You will have to come back."

Michiko glanced behind her. She could see something sticking out of their wooden slot, but there was no point in asking. Four o'clock was the only time that the woman would let her pick up the mail, and the clock said five more minutes.

"I'll just wait," Michiko said with a giant smile. It had become a bit of game with her. No matter how nasty the woman was to her, Michiko smiled back. It seemed to make the postmistress more miserable, though, which wasn't really the point.

The woman behind the wicket turned with an irritated flick of her hand, grabbed the letters from their slot, and slid them along the counter.

"Thank you," Michiko said as she picked them up. She prayed there wasn't any bad news. Every letter that came to their house seemed to bring nothing but that.

That evening, during a supper of sausages with onion and cabbage, the letters waited against the sugar bowl. Food always came first.

Finally, her father slit open the long grey envelope with his penknife and pulled out the paper. He scanned the single sheet, took a deep breath, and handed it to Eiko.

"It's approval for our permit!" she said, holding it to her heart. "I didn't think it would ever come. All we need now are our letters."

"What letters?" Michiko asked.

"Personal reference letters," Sadie said with a hint of coldness. She stabbed a piece of sausage with her fork in anger. "Letters that say 'this Japanese-Canadian family will not be a public burden.'"

"I'll take them to the RCMP tomorrow," Eiko said, reaching to take Sam's empty plate. "The owner of the drugstore has given you a fine reference. Mrs. Morrison has written one, and she talked her neighbour, Bert, into writing one for painting his barn."

"Not just me," Sam said as he opened the second letter. "Michiko and Clarence painted it as well." He scanned the pages of elegant handwriting. He didn't even try to read them, just handed them over to his wife.

Michiko's mother took the pages and read. Her face lost colour as she uttered the exclamation, "Oh, dear!"

"What's wrong?" Sadie asked.

Eiko read out loud. *"We have lost an employee and would like you to come as soon as possible. The flowers will soon be ready to harvest, and bulb retrieval will follow,"* she read. *"We will be able to accommodate you, but not your family until your quarters are made ready."*

Sadie gave a sharp cry. "What?"

Her mother lowered the letter to the table. "The rest is just new terms of employment."

"We'll have to change my train reservation," Sam said, taking the letter back. His furrowed brow gave him an anxious look.

"I'll take this letter along with the rest," her mother advised.

"Let's see it," Sadie said, holding out her hand. She scanned it quickly and handed it back to Sam. "At least your job's not as dangerous as the one Kaz hopes to get."

Michiko had swept the stairs for what she hoped would be the last time. She put down the dustpan and broom and sat for a rest. Her almost packed suitcase waited on the floor beside her bed, her dresser drawers empty and clean. All she had to do was put in her nightgown after she dressed in the morning. There were no new shoes to pack or wear.

Sadie had washed and rearranged most of the shelves in the drug store and was standing at the top of the ladder with a feather duster, cleaning the paddles of the ceiling fan, when Kaz arrived. Michiko was still a little shy of this tall bronze-skinned man with short black hair and chocolate eyes. Last year he had been her teacher, now he was her uncle.

"Jump," he said, seeing his wife on the ladder. "I'll catch you."

"Don't be silly," Sadie said crossly.

Michiko heard her come down the ladder. *If I remain quiet on the stairs, I just might find out about his dangerous job, the one Sadie doesn't want him to get.*

"Well," Sadie said with a great sigh, "tell me what happened."

"It was just as they said in the newspaper," Kaz said. "The British Command sent a recruiting officer to seek out candidates. Winston Churchill admonished Prime Minister Mackenzie King for the lack of *Nisei* in Canadian uniform."

Michiko knew that *Nisei* meant Japanese born elsewhere, unlike her father, who was *Issei*, born in Japan, and then came to Canada.

"How about that," Sadie said with heavy sarcasm. "Someone actually reprimanded our prime minster, the great Mackenzie King."

Michiko could hear her aunt tapping the floor with the toe of her shoe, something she did when she was nervous.

"Did you get accepted?" Sadie said.

"They don't want us," Kaz replied. "Present Canadian regulations do not permit *such personnel* to be enlisted in the Canadian Army."

"That is the best news I've heard all week," Sadie screeched. Michiko knew her aunt would throw her arms around him and kiss him. That always embarrassed her.

"I'm not going to give up," Kaz said seriously. "I filled in all the forms and told them to keep my name on file."

Michiko heard the squeak of one of the red stools at the soda fountain as he sat down.

"So what is our next move?" Sadie asked as the stool next to him creaked.

"There's still Alberta."

There was such a long pause, Michiko couldn't stand the suspense and put her head around the corner to see and hear better.

A dark splotch of blush had crept along her aunt's slender throat. "I won't be stoop labour in a beet field just so you can get into a uniform. That's the only job I'll get if we go to Alberta."

"It's not the uniform, and you know it."

Sadie jumped up and turned to him in anger. "Have you completely forgotten Hastings Park? It was the army that brought all the Japs in and cooped them up."

Kaz crossed his arms and leaned back in a position that suggested conversation was over until Sadie composed herself.

Sadie dropped back down onto the stool beside him. "After all the government has done to humiliate us, you still want to sign up. I just don't understand."

"The only one that can humiliate you is yourself," Kaz replied. He put his arm around her. "We talked about this before. I told you I was in agreement with the Japanese Canadian Citizen's League when they petitioned the government. They even paraded on the Powell Street baseball grounds to prove they were ready for action."

"But that was years ago, and it was just politics," she said in a low voice.

Kaz put his hands to her face and traced her cheek with his thumb. "Don't you understand? Instead of being part of the problem, I want to be part of the solution."

"I want things to go back to the way they were," Sadie said with a crackle of tears in her voice. "I want my old life back."

Kaz looked into Sadie's eyes. "We have to plan our life on what we have," he said, "not on what we are missing."

"But we have nothing, and I'm tired of building a life around nothing."

"Just remember," Kaz said, "better to bend than break." Then he pulled her into his arms.

Michiko, not wanting to see them kiss, went up the stairs with feet of velvet just as her grandfather had taught her.

The next day, her father left for his new job in Ontario. The force of the pelting rain scattered the last of the blossoms of the rose bush her mother had nurtured into bloom. Bruised, broken petals littered the ground as her father got into the RCMP car. Even though he had permission to leave the camp, it was too much like the last time, when the RCMP escorted the Japanese men to the train station and they hadn't seen him for a long, long time.

Chapter 4

GOODBYE, GHOST TOWN

The fat white cat, sitting in the sun with its tail wrapped about its feet, looked at Michiko and Hiro with its one green eye and one blue eye. Michiko put out her hand. The cat licked it with her rough tongue. Then it rose and waddled into the barn. Hiro followed.

"Don't go far," Mrs. Morrison said, making her way to the compost heap with a bucket of vegetable peels. "Your mother will be back soon."

Michiko bent to kiss the tiny forehead of her baby sister lying in her carriage. She loved the smell of her powdered skin. Hannah's face crumpled, and she gave out a small cry. "I'll walk her around," Michiko said. "That will keep her happy until Mother returns." *And when she does,* Michiko's heart gave a small leap of joy, *she will have our train tickets.* Her father's latest letter told them they were ready for them in Ontario. The whole family, except for Sadie and Kaz.

Hiro had left the barn by the time she pushed the baby carriage down the lane and back. Knowing her little brother was fond of hide-and-seek, she went inside Mrs. Morrison's house and looked behind the curtains, under the dining room table. Then she went upstairs to his usual places, but he wasn't to be found. *He's probably climbing the fence that keeps the cows from the road,* Michiko thought. From the moment her little brother could crawl, he had climbed stairs, chairs, and along the backs of settees. Then he climbed the trees in Mrs. Morrison's orchard.

"He wouldn't have gone far," Mrs. Morrison said when Michiko entered the kitchen, calling his name. "He hasn't had lunch yet." She wiped her hands on her apron and lifted Hannah from the carriage. The tiny dark-haired baby looked even smaller in Mrs. Morrison's large, work-worn hands. "I know how to get his attention," she suggested. "Just call him for lunch, and hungry Hiro will come."

Michiko smiled. Mrs. Morrison was right. In the orchard she yelled out, "Lunch time!"

Two small bare legs dangled down from one of the lower tree branches. "Here I am," Hiro called out. "I was watching my baby," he said as he landed on the grass with a soft plump and pointed to the small black-and-white ball of fur nestled into one of Hannah's blankets. "I found it in the barn."

Michiko looked down. There was only one kind of black-and-white furry animal that she knew, and they weren't to be bothered. She backed up and looked around the field. *Where there is a baby, there is a mother nearby.* She had learned that with bears on the road last year. Michiko took her brother's hand. "Let's run," she said.

Her mother sat with Mrs. Morrison at the kitchen table, sipping tea from china cups.

"There was a baby skunk in your barn," Michiko blurted out.

"Pardon me?" Mrs. Morrison said.

"Hiro picked it up and made a bed for it."

"That's odd," Mrs. Morrison said. "Skunks don't nest this close to town. Did you see it?"

"No, I just saw the baby. It's a tiny black-and-white thing, curled up in a ball."

"Did you shut the barn door?" Eiko asked Hiro.

Hiro gazed up and shook his head.

Eiko looked at Mrs. Morrison. "If he left the door open, maybe it will wander away."

"Not if she's got babies," Mrs. Morrison said. "Mother skunk will be searching for it, and she will not be happy." She put on her canvas gardening gloves, a pair of rubber boots, and picked up her stiff corn broom. "If I yell, break out the tomato juice."

Michiko looked at her mother and raised her brows, but her mother just smiled.

No sooner had she left than Mrs. Morrison was back.

"Hiro," she said as she stepped out of her boots, "show me where you put the baby cat."

"Cat," Michiko repeated. "It's a cat?" She jumped from her chair, ran out the kitchen door to the foot of the apple tree, and scooped up the tiny kitten.

In a shaft of afternoon sun the white cat prowled the earth floor of the barn, mewing.

"Here," she said, extending the small bundle to Mrs. Morrison.

"Just put it down," Mrs. Morrison said.

"Here you are!" Michiko whispered as she lowered the tiny body to the floor. Completely black, except for its tail, the kitten had a small drop of white on its nose like a splash of milk. Three other kittens, all white, lay on a pile of newspapers inside the wooden box.

The mother cat licked her baby from head to toe, and then, taking the scruff of its neck in her mouth, placed it next to its brothers and sisters.

Michiko reached out to stroke the mamma cat's back. "We'll have to help you raise your family," she said. "That's what good friends do."

When she looked up at Mrs. Morrison, the woman's eyes were filled with tears.

That night, Sadie and Kaz joined them for a farewell banquet of roast pork, vegetables, and mashed potatoes. An enormous loaf of bread with a buttered furrow along the top stood beside a dish of homemade pickles. In their honour, Mrs. Morrison had opened her last jar of red currant jelly. She followed the meal with a deep dish of apple crisp slathered with heavy cream and cups of strong black tea.

Michiko and Sadie did the dishes while their stout and generous friend rocked Hannah in the wooden chair in her kitchen.

"Why didn't George King's father go off to war?" Michiko asked in a voice low enough for her mother not to hear from the living room, where Kaz and Hiro played "horsie." George King talked a lot about fighting and taking sides. She wondered why his father was one of the few men in town.

Edna Morrison shifted the sleeping baby into Sadie's arms, poured herself a fresh cup of tea, and sank back into the rocking chair. Michiko listened to the wooden rockers thud against the hardwood floor for a few moments before Mrs. Morrison spoke. "You know George's mother was my best friend all through school."

"She was?' Michiko couldn't suppress her surprise.

"When she told me Robert King wanted to marry her, I tried to look pleased," she said. "That man was nothing but charm, hair grease, and a thin-lipped smile. But he always got what he wanted. After one year of marriage, my best friend became a woman who had to look at her husband before she could even ask the price of potatoes. I never liked that man."

Michiko looked up at Sadie, and they both grinned.

"He saw himself being far too important a man to enlist," Edna whispered. She chuckled. "I'll never forget the day my chickens came at him. Animals know who not to trust, you know."

Michiko wished they could take the upright concert piano, but it wasn't theirs to take. Even though her mother had reupholstered the threadbare stool, it had come with the apartment.

The security truck was making a special trip to the train station that next morning. Mr. Hayashi, the security officer, invited Mrs. Morrison to accompany Michiko's family, but she declined, which left space for Clarence. She had already said her goodbyes.

Sadie hung on to Michiko for so long, she hardly breathed, and then she released her and took Hannah into her arms. "You could leave her here with me," she said, nuzzling the little girl's head.

"You are welcome to keep Hiro," Michiko offered, which earned her a kick on the shins from the angry little boy.

Her mother took Hiro by the hand and led him over to Clarence. She took Hannah from Sadie's arms and placed her in their wicker laundry basket. "We don't want to miss our train," she said sharply.

Kaz loaded their possessions into the back of the truck, stood at Sadie's side, and put his arm around her.

They all waved until they were out of sight. As they passed the RCMP guardhouse, Michiko wondered if there would be one like it on the road of their new home.

The Kootenay Mountains came into view as they left town. In some places the pine trees marched right down the side of the mountain to the edge of the road, as if waiting to cross. Their branches grew right to the ground. Hiro would have climbed them like a ladder.

A sign for Arrow Lake Loggers pointed down a dirt road. "That's where your Uncle Ted works," her mother said, pointing it out to Hiro.

A white peak touched the only cloudless piece of sky. Michiko looked up to see a rectangular patch of ground carved out of its side, as if a giant had shaved a patch of beard. "See, Hiro," she said. "Uncle Ted is way, way up that mountain."

Bleached driftwood littered the white sandy shores of the deep green lake that appeared before them. Not a ripple, not a boat, not a person in sight; it was totally untouched.

"That water is real cold," Clarence said. "That's why there's no one swimming."

"Too cold for fishing?" Michiko asked.

"No lake is too cold for fishing," Clarence said, nudging Michiko.

Michiko gave a secret smile, thinking about the telephone conversation she had with her Uncle Ted when he called to say goodbye.

"What about your fishing equipment?" she had asked him, careful not to alert anyone on their party line to what was hidden in the branches of the fallen willow tree beside the creek.

"My old fishing rods, the ones I never use?" he asked, just as cautious.

"And that thing you keep them in," she said, "the apple crate?" That was the code name they used for the little red boat her uncle had named *The Apple*.

"Oh, that old thing," Ted said. She could hear the smile in his voice. "It's no good to me now. It's yours to give to whoever you want."

Clouds parted, and the sun lit the snow on the mountains. Michiko watched the cascading water along the roadside, wondering if the stream would follow them all the way to the station.

"Look down," Clarence told her when they saw the sign for Deep Creek.

Michiko couldn't see the bottom of the gorge.

The poker-straight pines that rocketed to the sky gave way to bush. Michiko wondered if Ontario had lots of trees. How big were their mountains?

After a few zigzags in the road, she spotted a faded sign for Frank's General Store on the side of a barn. They twisted and turned farther and farther from the ghost town, into the valley.

Willow trees appeared with jet-black cows munching grass beneath them. Soon Michiko could see low wooden houses with sheds. More cows dotted the foothills, and then the road turned from dust to gravel. They were in the town of Nelson.

Michiko placed her grandfather's old cardboard suitcase on the station platform. His letters lay inside Clarence's blue box. She had rescued them from the bin of materials her father was burning at the back of the drugstore.

The tough little bushes growing by the railway station were loaded with fat blueberries. Clarence ambled off and was soon back with a capful.

Michiko popped one into her mouth. "About your going away gift ..." she said.

Clarence furrowed his brows. "I thought you said you were making something."

"I did," Michiko replied. "But it didn't work out,

so I'm going to give you something that someone else made. It was just too big to carry."

Hiro sat on the edge of the wooden platform, watching a trail of ants crawl in and out of their sandy hill. "Look," he said with a smile. Michiko crouched beside him and pointed to a large black ant carrying a seed. "That is what Clarence will look like when he has to carry his present home," she said.

"I don't get it," Clarence said. "How come you think I'm going to be an ant?"

"I just hope you don't mind second-hand presents," Michiko said, getting up and dusting off the back of her dress.

"You are driving me crazy," Clarence said.

"Well," Michiko whispered, looking around to make sure no one was listening. "You remember the day we spent fishing with Kiko and George?"

Clarence nodded and opened his eyes wide. Who would forget the day George King almost drowned trying to spy on their fishing expedition?

"Mrs. King plans to inform the authorities about someone in the orchard owning a boat."

"I'm going to fix him," Clarence vowed, holding up a clenched fist, "as soon as I get back to town."

"When you get back to town, you are going to go to the King house and ask his mother if George can go fishing with you."

"Why am I going to do that?" Clarence curled back his lips and sucked through his teeth. "I'm going to punch him right in the face for squealing about your uncle's boat."

"You mean *your* boat."

"That's right," Clarence said, caught up in his anger. "First thing I am going to do is punch him in the face for squealing about my boat." He was just about to smack the palm of his hand with his fist when he stopped and looked at her in surprise. "*My* boat?" He turned red about the ears.

"That's why it's a second-hand gift," Michiko explained. "My Uncle Ted told me before we left it was mine. Now I am telling you before I leave that it is yours."

"You gotta be kidding," Clarence said. He plunked his hat down on top of his head with a face full of surprise. "I can't believe it," he said, slamming it down with his hand.

Hiro jumped up and clapped his hands. "Funny Clarence," he said as the blue juice from the berries dripped down his face and off the tip of his chin.

The pebbles along the tracks jumped and rattled as the locomotive pulled into the station. The train's shrill whistle startled Hannah into a cry as the white steam filled the platform. "Oh!" Eiko said, waving her hands back and forth in front of her face. "Hiro, do you feel the hot breath of that *kaibutsu*?"

She took her young son's hand as they mounted the metal steps. Michiko carried Hannah in their wicker laundry basket. Clarence and Mr. Hayashi helped with their luggage.

Their travelling space for the next three and a half days would be a sleeping compartment with its own toilet and sink. The maroon velvet curtains matched the plush covers of the wide, comfortable seats. The little dark-panelled drawing room was more expensive than the sleeping cars, but here they could keep to themselves.

Clarence pulled the upper berth down from the ceiling and whistled. He opened the door to the small washroom and smiled. "This would be perfect for my place."

Michiko bit her bottom lip and then said, "If I write to you, will you write back?"

"I guess," Clarence said, pulling his cap down over his eyes. "Not much good at it, though."

Mr. Hayashi stowed their belongings on the shelves designated for luggage. He shook her mother's hand and then reached into his pocket. "For the children," he said, placing two candies wrapped in gold foil into Eiko's hand.

Eiko touched his arm. "You have always been a great help," she said. "We will miss you."

From the window, Michiko watched the conductor pick up his little wooden step and put it inside the car. As the train lurched forward, she swung her arms as if she was hitting a ball. Clarence pretended to catch it. Then she waved until Clarence and Mr. Hayashi were out of sight.

Hiro squirmed all over the compartment as the train clattered out of the station. He wasn't interested in waving or looking at the dog that lay in the shade of a great tree oak beside the tracks. Michiko put her hands together and crossed her fingers, attempting to distract him. "These are mother's knives and forks," she recited, "and this is mother's table."

Hiro pushed away her hands. He turned to his mother's lap and pushed at the baby. "No more Hannah," he said.

"No, Hiro," Eiko said. "Hannah will stay in my lap for a while. You have your own seat."

Hiro threw himself at his mother's legs and then slid to the floor and rolled at her feet, wailing.

Michiko bent to lift him off the floor.

"Let him be," Eiko said. "He's just acting the way we all feel."

Michiko felt a cold clutch in her stomach watching her little brother shake with sobs.

After Hannah was fed, Eiko changed her diaper and put her back into her basket. "Now would you like to come up on my lap?" she asked her sad little son. Hiro crawled up onto the seat and laid his dark head on his mother's lap. The gentle rocking of the train finally put him to sleep.

The train moved out of the small town, past a sagging barn where a woman stood in front of a clothesline of billowing sheets, shading her eyes. She reminded Michiko of Mrs. Morrison, and she waved at her.

The woman waved back.

At first Michiko enjoyed looking out of the large window at white daisies that scattered the rough grass at the mountain edge. But before long the scenery became monotonous, nothing but towering rocks with pines in their crevices.

After the sun set, Michiko's mother pulled down the window shades and opened the hamper Mrs. Morrison had placed in the back of the truck. Her mother hadn't planned for them to eat in the car with tables set with white cloths and silver. Michiko was disappointed. She wanted to see the waiters hold the trays over their heads as they slid down the aisles, the way Sadie had described.

Mrs. Morrison's sandwiches had thick slices of pink ham with homemade mustard pickles. There were tiny tomatoes and radishes from her garden. Michiko bit her lower lip to hold back the tears. No longer would they visit the flower-filled farmhouse on the outskirts of town that smelled of cabbage and apple pie. After eating, Michiko reached into the hamper for the wax paper package of oatmeal cookies but drew back her hand in surprise.

"What's wrong?" Eiko asked.

"Something's making a scratching sound," she said, "like a mouse."

"I hope not," her mother said. "We've just eaten the food."

Michiko lifted the hamper and examined the bottom. "There's no hole," she said. When she placed the basket back on the floor, both heard the sound of a tiny mew.

"She didn't!" Eiko exclaimed as she pulled out the rest of the wrapped packages. A small white box punched with holes had the words "*Happy Birthday Hiro*" written across the top.

"Looks like she did," Michiko said as took out the box and undid the string that held the lid in place. She put her hands into the box and pulled out the tiny black-and-white kitten with a white drop on its nose.

"My baby," Hiro said as he scrambled across the seat.

The kitten wiggled from Michiko and jumped to the windowsill. Hiro's face lit up.

"Maybe she didn't pack it," Michiko said. "Maybe it just jumped in."

"And tied the string around the box afterward?" Eiko asked with a shake of her head. "She knew what she was doing." She removed a small jar of milk. "She packed dinner for it as well," she said with a small laugh. "Only Edna would think to do that."

The porter knocked on the door to turn their seats into beds.

Eiko swooped at the kitten, but it didn't want to give up its freedom, and it scampered to the windowsill. "Catch it," she whispered to Michiko, "they may put it off the train."

Michiko threw Hannah's blanket over top of the small animal and held it tight, hoping it wouldn't mew. When the porter left, she let it slide to the floor. Michiko filled the bottle's lid with milk and put it on the floor. The kitten crept closer with a rumbling purr.

Hiro moved to the pillow on his bed and lay down to watch. The kitten clambered up to him, nuzzled into the hollow of his arms, and went to sleep.

The steam whistle blew from the front of the train. *My life,* Michiko thought, as she lay in the top bunk, *is just like this train, always moving.*

Chapter 5

ARRIVAL

As the train pulled into the Toronto station, Michiko was dreaming that a photographer had asked her to pose as star pitcher for the Asahi baseball team. *"Look at that," Clarence was saying, holding the paper up for all to see. Then George King picked up a crayon, grabbed the paper, and gave her buck teeth, a moustache, and horns.* Michiko moaned and opened her eyes to a tunnel of darkness lit by yellow electric bulbs.

Not far from their railway car, her father waited on the platform in a pair of green working trousers and laced-up boots. She waved to him from the window, and he broke into a wide smile. Michiko scampered down to the station platform. He came to her, holding out his arms. Even though he was thinner, he felt solid and muscular.

Union Station was full of bustle and noise. Michiko could smell cinnamon biscuits, coffee, smoke, and perfume all at once, as her family walked through the cavernous space filled with long slants of early morning sun.

They passed people waiting on long wooden benches that reminded her of church pews. She followed her little brother's eyes up to the huge brass wall clock and the balcony overlooking the marble concourse. *Good thing Dad has a firm grip on his hand,* she thought. *He'd be up those stairs in a moment.* Her father's other hand grasped her mother's elbow as they followed the signs to the street. Two policemen watched them as they neared the exit. One of them touched the gun on his hip, as if he was making sure it was still there. Michiko held her breath and looked up at her father's dark chocolate eyes. They sparkled with pleasure, giving no sign of worry.

Michiko felt the rush of excitement from the crush of bicycles, buses, and streetcars when they exited the station. The smell of exhaust made her nose twitch. Beyond the entrance's granite columns, Michiko marvelled at the wide cement sidewalks, tall buildings, and church spires. Everything was so much bigger than what they'd left behind. All of the cars on the street seemed new. People fluttered about like flocks of birds, buying newspapers, gathering at bus stops, and hailing taxis. Michiko guessed this was the way it would be in Ontario and smiled at the thought of her whole life being bigger and busier.

Their new employer waited against the front fender of a long grey sedan, filling his pipe. He struck a match and then sucked on the stem to get it going. He held it for a moment and then exhaled a mouthful of smoke. A sturdy man with a ruddy complexion, Mr. Downey had large blue eyes with baggy skin beneath and bushy brows above. Seeing them arrive, he stepped forward to shake her mother's hand. "Hello, welcome to Ontario," he said in a deep but pleasant voice.

Hiro jumped behind his mother's skirt.

Sam took the front seat of the car, which smelled of tobacco smoke and pine air freshener. Michiko knew he wouldn't speak Japanese out of respect for his employer. The English words he occasionally mispronounced were like music to her ears.

The car wound its way past government and commercial buildings. Then they drove through streets of small red-brick houses, set close to the sidewalk with gardens full of geraniums and chrysanthemums. Vines crept up the sides of houses and grew over hydro poles. The car picked up speed when Mr. Downey turned on to a two-lane concrete road.

"It's a brand new road," her father told them, pointing out the small blue-and-yellow sign topped with a crown, "named after the queen."

Michiko glanced up at the double-armed light standards that separated the lanes of the highway. "Big lights," she said to Hiro.

"Not now," her father told them. "Blacked out for war."

"They said there'd never be enough cars to warrant a road like this," Mr. Downey added, "but there's traffic all the time." And he was right. Cars, trucks, even canvas-covered army vehicles passed them on the opposite side of the grassy boulevard.

Michiko admired the large, sprawling houses that sat beneath the shady trees growing beside this new concrete road. Eventually the city passed. Green fields and small stands of trees surrounded them. After pointing out a jam factory, an asparagus farm, and a mushroom barn, Mr. Downey slowed to a stop at a set of lights. He turned to them in the back seat and said, "I normally don't go home this way, but I need gas, and this way you will get to see the main part of town."

"Thank you," Eiko said as she rearranged Hannah, who was sleeping on her lap.

Mr. Downey turned off the highway and followed the gravel road into the gas station. As they waited for the attendant to fill the tank, he explained. "This part of the country is blessed with two magnificent harbours. The locals tie up at Bronte Harbour." He pointed out the coffee-brown river between high brown banks. "When we cross the bridge, you'll be able to catch a glimpse of something really big." He slowed the car down to give them a chance to see the large container ship that he called a "laker" tied up in the creek.

Michiko thought of Clarence's little red rowboat. *At least he won't have to hide it, like Uncle Ted did. I wonder if George will go fishing with him.*

Mr. Downey pointed out the Gregory Theatre. "Always plays the top movies of the day," he said. "They also host stage productions, if you enjoy that sort of thing."

Michiko craned her neck to see the marquee. *Too bad Aunt Sadie isn't here,* she thought as she rolled down the car window. She put her head out in anticipation of a real street of stores and wasn't disappointed. A church spire dominated the landscape of the downtown, and hydro poles towered over the three-storey brick buildings with colourful awnings that lined the long, busy main street. A five-and-dime store stretched the full length of a block. Next to it was Brown's Shoe Store. Michiko smiled. *There may be a chance of getting running shoes after all.*

At the corner, a sign reading TOBACCO hung over a window filled with glass containers and wooden pipes. Hiro clapped and pointed at the life-sized statue of an Indian chief in full headdress, clutching a handful of cigars. Everywhere there were advertisements for goods and medicines. Coca-Cola advertisements were painted on sides of buildings, standing in front of the stores, and in windows. Michiko counted three hardware stores and two restaurants. Dark sedans, with their noses to the sidewalk, filled both sides.

"Can we stop?" she asked.

"It's Saturday," her father said, "no place to park."

"What about there?" Michiko asked as they passed a large brick building with a deep green awning. It had no cars in front of it.

"Only if you have police business," Mr. Downey said with a laugh. "And if you park there without permission, you *will* have."

Sam laughed long and loud at what Mr. Downey said.

Michiko felt her face redden at her father, who was trying too hard to please.

The car slowed for a few seconds as Mr. Downey waved his arm at the small white stone building with the large number of bicycles in the rack beside the door. "If you like to read," he said, "that's the library."

Michiko was impatient to see where they would be living, but the main street moved farther and farther away. As they drove on, the shops disappeared altogether, and the number of houses dwindled. She slumped back into her seat and crossed her arms. "I thought we were moving to Oakville," she said in a low voice.

Eiko shook her head and put a finger to her lips.

Before long, the car turned down a road where several cows, all pointed in the same direction, stood behind a fence, their tails twitching in a continuous, swinging motion. Across the road, beside a sign marked *DOWNEY*, a wooden wheelbarrow filled with buckets of vivid red gladioli splashed the road with colour.

"Flowers are for sale," Sam turned in his seat to explain, "on honour system."

Michiko could tell the farmhouse they approached would be nothing like Mrs. Morrison's, with the broken fence that barely kept the meadow away, the flaking house paint, and string of ants that often wandered across her counter. Mr. Downey's neatly trimmed front lawn was the size of a baseball field. In the distance she could see a large barn and a shed surrounded by fields of bright, blooming gladioli.

The smell of freshly cut grass surrounded them as they stepped out of the car.

A walkway of worn bricks led from the main house to two small bungalows right past one of the biggest vegetable gardens Michiko had ever seen. She knew everyone in the ghost town had to slash away the crabgrass and thistles in order to plant a small patch of land. From dust to dawn, they bent over the hard, cracked soil weeding, hoeing, and carting water from the ground tap at the end of each street. But not one of them had a garden like this! If only Geechan could have seen this.

Mr. Downey removed the pipe from between his teeth and tapped it out against the car's back fender. "A small creek runs across the back of the property," he said. Then he pointed to the fields. "Everyone calls it a hundred and fifty acres," he said, "but it is really one hundred, forty-seven, and a half. You'll keep that little secret, I am sure," he said with a smile. "Hope you like apples," he added. "The trees in the back are all Spies."

What did he just say? Michiko had been so busy thinking about the gardens back home that she wasn't paying attention. *What did he say about spies and secrets?* She looked at her mother and father, but they didn't seem concerned.

Mr. Downey pointed out their new house and then touched the brim of his fedora, leaving Sam to show them inside.

Their little wooden house was not as big as Michiko had imagined. It was as if someone had taken the apartment from the drugstore and placed it on the ground. Its flat cement platform also served as the porch, with one step directly onto the grass.

As they entered the kitchen door, the smell of freshly painted walls greeted them. The house was clean, but its scrubbed stillness felt hollow.

Michiko breathed a sigh of relief at the sight of the fat porcelain faucets on either side of the kitchen tap.

Thank goodness they wouldn't have to pump water as they'd had to at the farmhouse in the ghost town. When the well froze, Michiko had had to drag water from the lake. She shivered at the thought of it.

A small, yellow-topped, metal table with four padded chairs stood on a floor of beige linoleum. Her mother removed the fly swatter from the table and placed it on the ledge of a window. The curtains hung from a thin wire.

A calendar that read "With Glad Compliments of Downey's Flower Farm" and a picture of a huge basket of gladioli hung on the wall. Beside it was a photo of Joe DiMaggio, clipped from a magazine.

"Look," Sam said. He put down the suitcases and walked to the tall wooden box against the wall. "We have an electric ice-box!"

"You mean refrigerator." Eiko corrected her husband with a wide smile and opened the door. A loaf of bread sat next to a brick of butter and a block of cheese.

"We have electric stove, too," Sam said, pointing to the range. The wire rack standing on the burner told Michiko they would be able to have toast.

Eiko pulled down the oven door and peered inside. "This will need a good clean," she said with a grimace.

Her father switched on an ugly brown radio with dusty grooves that radiated around the speaker. It sat on the counter beneath the white, paint-thickened cupboard doors. "Look, Hiro," he said, turning it around for him to see the tubes of red filaments. "We can get stations from the USA!" He turned the radio back and fiddled with the dial until he found a baseball game.

Hiro smiled.

"Is it allowed?" Michiko asked. For so long, radios had been forbidden to the Japanese.

Her father patted her on the head. "Everything is okay here," he said. "No worries."

They moved into the large front room. Eiko walked around, touching the mismatched furniture with the tips of her fingers. A large sofa covered in dark brocade held the shape of people who had sat in it year after year. A squat table with clawed feet stood between two upholstered chairs in front of the window. Eiko drew back the stiff beige curtains, and the room flooded with sunshine. Finally, she smiled.

The main bedroom held a double bed, a large six-drawer dresser, and a wardrobe. Eiko opened the wardrobe to reveal several empty metal hangers. A faint musty odour came from its rose-papered walls. Eiko opened the drawers of the bureau and sniffed. She removed the sheets of newspaper used for lining, crumpled them into a ball, and handed them to her husband.

The next bedroom had a crib and small cot. Michiko walked into the last room that had a single bed and sighed in relief. This room had a bookcase and a small table with a wooden chair.

Sam tapped the table. "Good place to study," he said with a grin. The movement made the goose-necked lamp wobble.

The bathroom was at the end of the hall. Except for the pink and white kitchen, every room in the house was pale green.

Their first meal was a bowl of tomato soup and a cheese sandwich.

"You'll be taking your lunch to school," Eiko said as she pushed a piece of paper and pencil toward Michiko. "Help me do a shopping list."

No one even suggested Japanese food.

Chapter 6

DEAR CLARENCE

Michiko lay quietly for a moment in the warmth of her new bed, listening to the morning sounds of a closing bedroom door, the flush of the toilet, and the gentle murmur of her parents talking. She rose, dressed, and went to her window, surprised at the absence of mountains. The view that stretched before her seemed to be nothing but sky and field.

A man in a black wool sweater, black corduroy trousers, and gardening boots was raking leaves. Curly black hair peeked out from the back of a cap pulled down over his ears. His hands were as thick and wrinkled as an old tree stump. The man stopped raking and looked up into one of the trees, revealing a large black moustache that made Michiko giggle. The skin crinkled around his eyes, and all his fierceness disappeared. Whatever the man saw in the tree made him smile.

Michiko craned her neck to see what was so amusing, but she couldn't. Her attention went to a slight woman in a faded housedress and headscarf walking toward the man. She carried a basket filled to the brim with tomatoes. The morning sun caught the heavy gold cross that hung from her neck.

Michiko's mother had told her another family lived and worked on the farm. Mr. Palumbo did the same job as her father, while his wife took care of the garden.

Michiko glanced in the direction of the vegetable patch. Near the wooden gate was a standpipe with a coil of hose. Beside that was a large green watering can. Most people thought gardening was an easy job, but Michiko knew how hard Geechan had worked on his tepees of beans, lines of carrots and onions, and rows of tomato plants. He had to hoe, water, pull weeds, and tie up stragglers. He even rose before the sun just to pick off slugs with his chopsticks.

Michiko turned from the window to the small table that served as her desk. Next to her jar of paper flowers was a stationery set from Sadie and Kaz, Clarence's blue box, and the sketch pad and package of coloured pencils Mrs. Morrison had given her.

She had three thank-you notes to compose. Michiko knew her mother's expectations, and it wasn't polite to delay in writing one's appreciation. She pulled out the chair just as Hiro raced into her room and threw himself on her bed, face down.

"What's wrong?" she asked.

"Mrs. Morrison's gone," came the muffled reply.

"What did you say?" Michiko asked.

"Mrs. Morrison's gone," he repeated.

"I know," she said. "Don't you remember waving goodbye?"

"My cat," Hiro wailed. "She's gone."

Michiko had to grin. Last night her father had told Hiro that the cat should have a name. "Did you forget to close your bedroom door?"

"No," Hiro said unconvincingly.

"She has to be somewhere in the house," Michiko assured him.

Hiro rolled over and sat up. "She ran home to her mother."

"That's too far away," Michiko said as she shooed him out the door. "Go have your breakfast while I write my letter. Then I will help you search." Just as she turned back to her desk, Michiko noticed Mr. Palumbo walk by with a ladder.

Dear Clarence,

You were right about the long train ride, but we had an extra passenger to entertain us. Mrs. Morrison packed one of her kittens in our food basket!!!!

To make the point of how surprised they all were, she added several more fat exclamation marks at the end of the sentence.

Our new house is small, but at least I have my own room.

Michiko thought about crossing that out to stop Clarence from thinking she was bragging; he shared his house with six other siblings. But she decided to leave the sentence in. She wished she had some great adventure to write about rather than the dullness of her life.

There is another house behind us with an Italian man and woman. Their son used to work on the farm, but he left for another job in Toronto. That's why my dad had to come early.

Thank you for the box. I'm going to keep letters in it, so you have to write back.

After signing it, Michiko folded the paper in half and stuffed it in the envelope. On the front she printed his name and address. On the back she printed her new one.

"One down and two to go," Michiko said as the smell of toast beckoned her into the kitchen.

Hiro sat at the table with his head in his hands, his toast untouched.

"I said I'd help you find her," Michiko said. "Eat up."

"Dad's gone," Hiro said.

Michiko looked at her father's empty chair and then up at her mother. "Dad's gone?" It was Saturday, and she had expected he would be spending the whole day with them.

"He'll be back," Eiko said. "He left at dawn to take a shipment of flowers to Toronto."

Michiko lifted her piece of toast to her mouth and thought about Toronto. She wondered if she would ever get a chance to go back there. Maybe she would be able to find Kiko, one of her classmates who had moved there last year. Michiko was just about to take a bite when there was a rap at the kitchen door. Her mother moved to open it, but before she reached the handle, it flew back and banged against the wall.

The thin old woman she'd seen through the window stood in the doorway.

"Buon giorno," she said as she stepped inside. Since she was no longer wearing her headscarf, Michiko could see her iron-grey hair, braided and pinned into a thick coil at the back of her neck.

"Mrs. Palumbo?" Eiko asked. She wiped her hands on her apron and extended one.

"*Si*," said the woman, but she did not take the offered hand. She stared at the two children the way an eagle sees its prey and then gave a smile that revealed two rows of brown teeth. With a spotted, gnarled finger, she beckoned to them.

"You want the children to come outside?" Eiko asked.

"*Si*," said the woman, putting out her hand.

Hiro fled from the table to hang on to his mother's skirt.

Michiko looked to her mother for direction. She didn't want to be rude, but she couldn't get rid of the feeling that she had just become Gretel while Hansel hid behind his mother's skirt. "Go on," Eiko said firmly. "See what she wants."

Michiko slid from her chair and put her hand out for Hiro to take.

He moved back farther against the wall.

Michiko shrugged and followed the woman outside and around the back of the house. Her feet sank into the soft grass, damp with early morning dew. Mr. Palumbo was coming down the ladder, cradling a tiny black cat with a white tail.

"Mrs. Morrison!" Michiko cried out as she reached to take the cat. "You found her!"

The woman knitted her brows in puzzlement. "Palumbo," she said, patting her chest, "*Signora* Palumbo."

Michiko nodded. "Thank you, Mrs. Palumbo," she said. "The kitten belongs to my brother. He was sad when he couldn't find her."

Mr. Palumbo nodded. Then he reached out, scratched the kitten's tiny head, and broke into a smile. Michiko took a closer look at his well-trimmed, heavy moustache and giggled. "Thank you," she said again.

The man doffed his cap and turned to remove the ladder as Michiko dashed back into the house. She placed the kitten into Hiro's arms.

"Mr. Palumbo found her up the tree," she explained. "He got a ladder to get her down."

Hiro drew the kitten to his face and nuzzled its fur.

"He should go outside and say thank you," Michiko said to her mother.

Hiro put the kitten on the floor next to its saucer of milk.

"Maybe he should write a thank-you letter," Michiko muttered as she returned to her toast. *At least this morning's adventure will give me something to write to Mrs. Morrison,* she thought. *Wait until she finds out Hiro named the kitten after her.*

The kitchen door swung open for a second time. It was her father.

"Where did you get that?" Eiko asked Sam, staring at the huge burlap bag in her husband's arms.

Sam put the rice sack on the counter. "A Japanese fellow gave me directions to his grocery store in Toronto," he said with a wide grin. "He says he'll stop by soon on his way to Niagara Falls."

"How much was it?"

"I got it on credit," he said sheepishly.

"On credit," her mother said, glaring at the bag as if it was garbage. "We never buy things on credit. What were you thinking?"

Sam's eyes went as hard as coal. "I was thinking of rice," he said, letting the screen door slam as he headed back outside.

Eiko looked at the door and shook her head.

"Rice!" Michiko exclaimed as she raced to the counter to examine the bag. She couldn't wait for its buttery, nutty smell to bubble up from the pot on the stove.

Chapter 7

SCHOOL

Mr. Downey drove an anxious Michiko and her mother into the village Monday morning. School had already started, and she had missed the first few weeks.

White trellises of late summer roses stood between the windows of the two-storey brick building. The well-manicured lawns boasted beds of geraniums and marigolds.

"It's so beautiful," Michiko murmured as they pulled up the drive. Her last school, a derelict hardware store in an abandoned part of the ghost town, had a dank, woody odour, and nothing was in bloom anywhere near.

"The Bronte Horticultural Society holds their meetings here," Mr. Downey said. "They oversee the landscaping in exchange. Turned out quite pretty, don't you think?"

Several children moved toward the entrance to stare at Michiko and her mother as they made their way up the walkway. Eiko ignored them as she marched into the building. Michiko, in her crisp white blouse, new skirt, shiny hair, and scrubbed face, waited on a chair in the school office with her lunch sack in her lap. She stared up at the glass cabinet filled with trophies, silver cups, and statues of men swinging bats. When the school bell rang, the building echoed with children's voices coming from every direction.

"I wish to enrol my daughter," Eiko said.

A man turned to look at her through glasses that caught the light and shone like mirrors. He removed the wire-framed spectacles, pulled a handkerchief from his breast pocket, and began to polish them. "I'm the principal, Mr. Nott," he said. "What was the last school she attended?"

"It was a private school," her mother responded with her head held high. "She began her education in Vancouver before we moved to a small town. The following year she transferred from the village school to a private institution." No mention was made of the fact that their non-government school was only for Japanese students. Michiko's mother handed the principal a sheaf of papers.

"Her marks are quite good," the principal commented as he riffled through the documents. "I assume you also have a birth certificate?"

Her mother opened the clasp of her black leather bag, removed it, and handed it to him.

Mr. Nott studied the certificate with a frown. "Your daughter appears to have two different names," he said. He looked over to Michiko. "Why is that, young lady?"

Michiko stood and shot to attention. "I used my Japanese name in Japanese school, and my English name in English school," she said with a nervous glance in her mother's direction.

The principal sorted through the reports, selected one, and handed the certificate back to Eiko. "Well," he said, "this is an English school, and therefore we will use your English name." He opened his desk drawer, removed a piece of paper, and pushed it toward Eiko. "Fill this out, please, while I take your daughter to class."

She nodded and picked up a pen.

"This way," Mr. Nott said to Michiko as he strode into the foyer.

Michiko waved to her mother and followed the principal to the last classroom in the corridor. He pushed open the door without knocking and swept his eyes across the rows of desks facing the chalkboard.

The teacher rose from her desk. The students jumped from their seats and chanted, "Good morning, Mr. Nott."

"Miss Barnhart, you have a new student," Mr. Nott boomed across everyone's heads. "Do you need a desk for …?" he hesitated, looked at the paper in his hand, and said, "Millie."

Michiko didn't have to look around to know she was the only one in the classroom with a Japanese face; the raised eyebrows and whispers behind hands told her. For a brief moment, she considered turning on her heel and running away. Instead, she raised her eyes to the samples of cursive writing on large green cards that marched across the top of the blackboard. Then she watched the thin red hand of the large clock next to the Canadian flag jerk past the minute lines.

The teacher shook her head. "No, thank you, Mr. Nott, we have an extra desk," she said. A necklace of seed pearls peeked between the turquoise buttons of her sweater set, and dark-framed glasses hung from a silver chain. Her blond hair formed a twist above the nape of her neck.

Miss Barnhart gestured that Michiko was to come to the front of the room. "You may sit here until I determine your reading group," she said, indicating Michiko was to take the stool beside her desk.

Michiko sat with the heels of her shoes resting on the bottom rung, proud she had not one spot of white polish on the brown sides of her saddle shoes. She arranged her new three-tiered flounced skirt with care and looked up to see some of the students whispering behind their hands.

"As always on Monday morning, we begin with current events," Miss Barnhart announced as she tapped the blackboard with her pointer. "Are there any new wartime regulations?"

Several hands shot up.

"Betty?"

"Don't serve bacon and eggs together," a girl in a plaid cotton dress said.

"And why is that?"

Betty lifted her head with pride and said, "It's one too many proteins on a plate. Our farmers have to feed the troops as well."

Miss Barnhart took a piece of chalk from the ledge and handed it to Betty. "You may record that," she said, turning back to the class and pointing to a blond boy with a brush cut in the third row.

Betty wrote out the new wartime regulation in large, loopy letters.

"Hitch a ride to save gasoline," Richard said.

The teacher nodded, and Betty handed Richard the chalk.

"One more," the teacher said. "Kenneth?"

"In winter, we should keep furnaces low and wear long underwear."

Everyone, including Michiko, laughed. While Kenneth was at the chalkboard, some students continued to snicker behind covered mouths.

"And to finish up," Miss Barnhart said, "what is our motto?"

Together the class chanted. "Use it up, wear it out, make do, or do without."

Michiko had to smile. Her family had lived by that motto even before the war began.

The teacher moved into the centre of the rows of desks. "Please stand if you have brought something to contribute to the war effort."

Several students shuffled to their feet.

"Donald," Miss Barnhart called out.

A boy in a striped T-shirt and blue jeans held up a bundle of newspapers tied with twine.

Miss Barnhart nodded, and he took them out the door.

Dorothy, from the middle of the classroom, held up a flattened tin can. The teacher nodded, and she placed it in a cardboard carton at the back of the room.

Miss Barnhart turned to a girl with long, dark hair, holding a lace handkerchief. "Carolyn," she asked, "what have you brought?"

Carolyn gave her hair a toss before she spoke. "I read that the army can make thirty bullets from just one of these." She held up an object wrapped in the white lace handkerchief.

The boys repeated the phrase "thirty bullets" in awe. Those at the back stood up to see better.

"Of course, I had to remind my mother every single day not to throw it out."

The suspense in the room built as the children craned their necks to see.

"Show it to us," the teacher said.

Carolyn cupped her free hand over the small white bundle and lifted her chin. "I thought I would make everyone guess."

The teacher's eyes flashed. "We don't have time for a game," she said, putting out her hand to receive the object. "Show us now, or we'll have to look at it during recess."

Carolyn's bottom lip protruded as she unwrapped the handkerchief and held up the small metal object. All eyes strained to see.

"One of my mother's lipstick tubes is made out of solid brass," Carolyn announced with excitement. "Just think, it will make thirty cartridges."

"Wow," said one of the boys at the back.

There was a brief spatter of applause and a few whistles. Carolyn faced the class with a large smile, gave a curtsey, and turned to the teacher. "I believe that qualifies me as being this week's top contributor," she said.

"We will still vote," the teacher said as she turned to the class. "Please raise your hand in favour of Donald's effort."

Most of the boys raised their hands.

"Please raise your hand for Dorothy's tin can."

Dorothy's hand shot up, and after glaring at the girl beside her, her hand shot up as well.

"And for Carolyn's brass lipstick tube?"

The rest of the class put up their hands.

"It seems we have a tie," the teacher said. She turned to Michiko. "Would you like to vote?"

Michiko nodded and stood up. "I think the boy with the newspapers did the most work," she said. "He had to go out and collect them. The girls just waited for something to be empty."

The girls in the classroom gave a collective gasp, while the boys cheered.

"Very good," the teacher said with a fox-like smile. "You considered working over waiting." Miss Barnhart turned to the class. "Millie understands the true meaning of the words 'war effort.'"

Michiko smiled, but the smile dropped from her face when she saw the dark look that Carolyn directed toward her.

"Please open your readers to the assigned page," Miss Barnhart told the class as she sat at her desk. "Can you read?" she asked kindly as she lifted her glasses to her nose.

Michiko nodded.

The teacher selected a passage from the first of three books sitting on top of her desk. She pushed it toward Michiko. "Begin anywhere," she said.

Michiko read passages in all three of the cloth-covered books with ease.

"You may sit beside Mary," Miss Barnhart said, handing her the reader with the blue cloth cover. She turned to the girl who had brought the lipstick tube. "Carolyn, please gather your things and move to the row behind."

"But Miss Barnhart," Carolyn said, narrowing her eyes, "you know Mary won't be able to concentrate without me."

"Carolyn Leahey," the teacher said, crossing her arms, "I thank you for moving."

Carolyn looked around at the other children and smirked. "Well, don't blame me if she doesn't do well," she said as she flung herself into the desk behind.

Michiko held her breath as she took her seat. *She talks like that to the teacher?*

Mary, the girl she was to sit beside, had soft curls that floated like a cloud of brown sugar around the yellow ribbon she wore as a headband. Just below her sky-blue eyes, a small dusting of freckles danced across her tiny nose. She wore a full-skirted dress of yellow with a white sweater draped over her shoulders. A chain of daisy clips held it in place.

Michiko was thankful she had brushed her hair a hundred times that morning.

"The Robins Reading Group," Miss Barnhart informed her, "are on page fourteen. Your questions are on the first chalkboard in front of you. Did you bring any school supplies, Millie?"

Michiko shook her head. Nothing would be purchased until her mother knew exactly what was needed, but she was too embarrassed to say. "I wasn't sure...." she mumbled.

"You can stay in at recess, and I will help you make a list," Miss Barnhart said, returning with a sharpened pencil, a small pink eraser, and a few sheets of foolscap.

Michiko read the assigned story and concentrated on answering the questions. She finished in time for the teacher to announce recess.

"Is she Chinese?" she heard someone ask as they headed out the door.

"I've never had a Chink in my class before," said another.

Michiko turned to the beginning of the reader to catch up on what she had missed. *Let them think I'm Chinese. It might be better for everyone.*

"Bus students eat lunch in the art room across the hall," Miss Barnhart told her at the beginning of the lunch break. Michiko removed the lunch sack from her desk and walked to the room across the hall. A handful of students sat at the large, wide tables. She went to the end.

"What farm are you from?" a small, shrill voice called out to her from across the room.

Michiko looked up.

A young girl wearing a faded chequered dress spoke to her from the doorway. Her tousled yellow hair reminded Michiko of a dandelion. "If you eat in the lunchroom, you hafta live on a farm, right?"

Michiko nodded as she unwrapped her cheese sandwich and raised it to her mouth.

"She probably doesn't speak any English," someone said, "like the *Eye-ties*."

Michiko put down her sandwich. "My family lives on the flower farm owned by Mr. Downey," she said to no one in particular.

"That's right across the road from our place," a boy's voice said.

Michiko turned to the blond boy in a plaid shirt and faded jeans. His sandwich bread showed bright against his dirty fingernails. He was in her class, but she wasn't sure of his name.

"Where the cows are?" she asked.

"Yep," the boy said. "But it's not a whole herd, it's just a few head for our own use. We get to drink all the milk we want."

"My little brother likes cows," Michiko said.

"Bring him over," the boy said. "He can help me milk them."

Michiko smiled, remembering the time Hiro tried to help Mrs. Morrison milk her goat. More milk ended up on him than in the pail.

The little girl who had first spoken to her left her table and went to the boy in the plaid shirt. Michiko noticed the hem of her dress was beginning to unravel. Her faded socks puddled around her ankles.

"Ask her where's she's from," her small voice insisted.

"Meet my nosy sister," the boy said. "Her name is Annie. Mine's William, but everybody calls me Billy, Billy Agar."

"I'm Mich—" she began to say but stopped. The principal had introduced her as Millie, and she might as well go back to it. "I'm Millie," she said before taking another bite of her sandwich.

A bit later, Annie followed Michiko out on to the playground, but Michiko didn't want to be bothered with this little girl; she wanted to watch the group of boys tossing a baseball around the diamond. She moved in their direction and sat down on the nearby swing. Billy was pitching. *He seems to have a good arm,* she thought.

Annie hopped onto the swing beside her and twisted herself around until the chains were tight. Then she spun round.

A small group of girls from her classroom formed a huddle near the door. Soon they were pointing at her. Michiko noticed that none of them were interested in the baseball game.

The shrill tweet of a factory whistle startled her, and she stopped pumping.

"We're supposed to go in when the whistle blows," Annie said as the boys in the field moved toward the door.

Michiko leapt from the swing and ran for the doors. She'd have to find out how to get on the team.

Chapter 8

THE TRAVELLING GROCERY TRUCK

Hannah's small cry brought her mother's footsteps into the room across the hall, but it was too early for Michiko to get up. She rolled over to face the wall. Then she remembered Mr. Downey had promised to take them to the basket factory and threw back the covers.

Her father took his shirt from the ironing board, pulled it on, and buttoned it up. Michiko wondered at times why he bothered with a shirt at all. Within minutes it would be off, and he would work the rest of the day in his singlet. She could see the tanned outline of it when he washed at night. He poured himself a cup of coffee from the percolator on the stove.

"You drink coffee?" Michiko asked in amazement.

"Boss drinks it," he said, taking a small sip and grimacing.

"I think you're supposed to add milk and sugar," Michiko said, "like Mrs. Morrison."

Sam opened the door of the refrigerator and removed a small bottle of milk. "Welcome to the land of milk and honey," he said, as he changed the black surface of his drink to a soft brown. He lifted the lid of the glass bowl and spooned out some sugar. He took a second small sip and pursed his lips. "Better," he said.

Her father's summer work of cutting and delivering flowers would soon be over as they moved into the fall season. He told her that his next job would be digging up the bulbs and sorting them. Mr. Downey sold all his gladiola bulbs for thirty-five cents a dozen, or three dollars for a hundred, all but those that went back into the ground and the ones from the plant that won him first prize each year in the annual show. Her mother had pointed out the row of first prize silver vases that stood along Mr. Downey's mantle.

As they stepped out the front door, the rumbling of an old delivery truck made her father smile. Naggie Fujioka had kept his promise and stopped his travelling grocery truck on the way to Niagara Falls. Her mother came out of the house clutching Hannah with one arm and her purse in the other. Hiro followed.

"Welcome, new people," the driver of the truck said as he jumped from the cab and waved his arms about. "I know all Japanese families in Great Golden Horseshoe." Naggie opened the truck's wide back doors and pulled down a wooden step for them to mount.

Michiko liked the idea of living in a golden horseshoe. It sounded so much better than ghost town.

"Come in, come in," the thin Japanese man repeated, giving a huge smile of dark gums and broken teeth. His sleek, flat head and narrow eyes reminded Michiko of a weasel. He wore a white shirt rolled to the elbows. His dark baggy pants, shiny from too much wear, clung to his thin, marble-like knees.

Eiko took a deep, purposeful breath and mounted the steps carrying her purse. Michiko and Hiro followed her into the dim interior of the truck. They were immediately assailed by the acrid odours of raw fish, overripe vegetables, and musty dried mushrooms. Hiro made a face and climbed back outside. For a fleeting minute Michiko felt sad, remembering these kinds of smells from her visits to her grandparents on Powell Street.

The slanted bins that ran along one side of the truck held the kind of vegetables her family liked: bean sprouts, bok choy, *nappa*, and the hairy roots of ginger and white radish. Below the bins, open wooden barrels held different coloured beans. A large tub filled with lumps of creamy white tofu and one of red bean paste sat at the back. Huge stacks of rice sat at the sides. Cast iron skillets, pails, and scrub brushes hung from nails on the wall behind.

On the opposite side of the truck, shelves held packages of noodles, green leaf tea, sesame seeds, and crackers. The shelf below held assorted tins, bottles of *shoyu*, and vinegars. Below the shelves were large ice chests, painted with black Japanese letters.

Her mother lifted the lid of one of the ice chests; several fish lay on top.

"You like eel?" the man asked after she put the lid down. "Eel good price today," he said, pointing to the chest beside it. "Also have," he said, rubbing his hands together, "shrimp and oyster."

"A couple of those mackerels will do," her mother said as she moved to the shelves.

Michiko lined up her mother's purchases on the small counter next to a metal scale and cash register. Next to the ginger root that reminded Michiko of a little old man, she placed a long head of wrinkly cabbage, a small bag of dried mushrooms, and a package of dried seaweed. A large chunk of white tofu floated in a small pail of water. Next to that were a bottle of soya sauce, a ball of miso in wax paper, and a jar of pickled plums.

"The plums are for your father," Eiko said with a grimace after the shopkeeper placed them on the counter. She spotted a stack of small bars of soap wrapped in rice paper and put her fingers to her mouth in thought. Then she reached out, took one, and placed it on the counter. "This will be for me."

Michiko lifted the soap to her nose. Her aunt Sadie always smelled of flowers, a fragrance that often stayed behind after she had left the room. The soap's familiar sandalwood fragrance brought her a sense of contentment.

"First time I charge for pail and tofu," the grocer said as he calculated the cost. "Next time you bring pail and just pay for tofu." He gave a huge grin of broken teeth and said, "I no charge for water."

"Don't forget we owe you for a bag of rice," Eiko said, opening her purse.

"You not worry," the man said. He put on a pair of small, round glasses and flipped through a worn leather journal next to the cash register. "I have husband's name in book."

"You can cross it out," Eiko said as she placed several one-dollar bills on the counter. "We keep our accounts paid."

The man shrugged and reached for the pencil behind his ear.

Her father peeked through the door. "Ready to head out?"

Oakville Wood Specialities, a brick and concrete building sheathed in corrugated metal, sat beside railroad tracks surrounded by piles of logs. Trails of white steam rose from several roof stacks as they approached. Even though it was Saturday morning, the factory teemed with workers. Men moved back and forth, loading the boxcars.

"Mr. Downey," Michiko asked, "how many baskets do you need?"

"I'm here for the sawdust," he said. "We'll be needing plenty of that soon, for the bulbs. I get a good price on firewood too. They're happy to get rid of the cores after the veneer is gone. "

Mr. Downey led Michiko and her father up the gravelled drive to the main building. "All the baskets are made by hand," he said. He greeted a short, dark-haired man with a handshake. "Hello, Hank," he said. "Mind if these folks have a look around?"

Hank wore a diamond-patterned wool vest over his long-sleeved shirt. His scuffed work boots seemed out of place with his well-creased flannel pants.

"Go on in," he said, looking Sam up and down. "You looking for work?"

Mr. Downey gave the man a small jab with his elbow. "Knock it off," he said and then turned to Sam. "Most of the young men don't want to spend their life working on a farm," he said. "Between this factory and the war, it's hard to find men to work the fields."

Michiko couldn't help but think of her Uncle Ted. He was always interested in anything made of wood, and Uncle Kaz was having a great deal of trouble finding the right job. If they got both got jobs at the basket factory, the whole family could be together again. "We know some people ..." she said, but Sam grabbed her hand. The pressure he put on her fingers told her he was unhappy with her interruption. "This is adult business," he said to her in a low voice. "You stick to kid business."

The four of them stepped through the large-planked doors that stood ajar. Inside, dust motes danced through the rays of sunshine that rested on the heads of the men working at tables.

Several worked at a machine shaving logs into long thin strips. It reminded Michiko of her mother preparing potatoes. Others carried bundles of the peeled wood to a huge vat of steaming water. Men at a long work table shaped wet strips over small wooden blocks and hammered in tacks. Then they positioned a strip of wood along the top edge and stapled it.

"Even though berry season is over," Hank said, as he picked up a small box with a wide square opening, "we got to keep up the stock." He turned the box over, examined its base, nodded, and handed it back.

They moved to the men at the next table. For several minutes, Michiko watched the workers mould pieces of veneer over metal forms. *It's as if they are doing origami with wood,* she thought to herself. After adding a solid oval piece to the bottom and stapling inner and outer bands to the top, another sweet-smelling wooden basket joined the pile.

"I'll take my usual order of six quarts for my apple crop," Mr. Downey said. "And I'll need some pints for my strawberries."

"I'll put it on your bill," Hank replied as they moved from the factory to the office of the assistant general manager. On the wall behind his desk was a framed photograph of a warplane.

"See that, Sam?" Mr. Downey said. "The factory produces veneer for propellers as well. It's doing its part for this darn war."

Sam barely glanced at the photograph. Michiko knew he did not want to be reminded of the war that had removed them from their home.

Mr. Downey gave his order for winter wood and sawdust. He stuffed his copy into his back pocket and turned to them. "Now," he said, "we can get your wife a basket." He strode off toward a set of wooden stairs that led up the side of the building.

Sitting in a dusty corner on the second floor of the factory were two wooden benches. On one sat a set of simple tools. On the other was a small, thin man.

"I could have picked you up a basket myself," Mr. Downey said. "But I thought you would like to meet Mr. Takahashi. Market baskets are his speciality."

The Japanese man on the bench rose slowly, brushed the knees of his pants, wiped his fingers on a cloth, and extended his hand to her father.

Sam took the man's hand in both of his and pumped it up and down. "Happy to meet you," he said with a large grin.

Michiko held her breath. *Will they begin to speak Japanese? If they do, will it be all right, or will my father get in trouble?*

"I think," Mr. Downey said, "it would be easier for both of you to speak in private, if you know what I mean." He looked at Michiko, winked, and left.

Michiko's father grinned from ear to ear as he launched into a lengthy spatter of Japanese words that were returned with equal enthusiasm and speed. It seemed as if they would talk forever, until Mr. Takahashi moved to his place on the empty bench and to Michiko's great surprise grabbed a handful of tacks from the bucket at his feet and tossed them into his mouth.

She watched the small Japanese man shape and weave several splints of wood around a rectangular block of wood, tacking them neatly in place with his hammer. Mr. Takahashi's hand moved from his mouth to the basket so fast, it was as if he was a machine himself. Using a small set of shears, he nipped the edges of the splints to make them even and attached two more strips of wood for trim. These were of darker and heavier veneer than the woven bed.

After he attached the handle, Mr. Takahashi spat the last of the tacks into his hand, tossed them back into the bucket, and handed Michiko the basket.

She ran her hand across the bottom and along the insides and then put it over her arm. Michiko knew how much her mother valued handmade items that showed care and precision. "*Arigato*," she said quietly.

Mr. Takahashi gave a bouncing kind of nod and smiled.

Sam reached into his pocket and removed several dollar bills, but Mr. Takahashi waved his hands about his head, refusing to touch them. Her father and the basket maker argued back and forth in Japanese until Sam put the money away. They shook hands and spoke some more. Michiko had absolutely no idea what was discussed, but she had not seen her father smile as long or as broadly in a very long time.

That night, Michiko waited in anticipation as her mother filled their bowls with hot rice and placed a strip of steaming fish on top.

"*Itadakimasu*," she whispered before they began their meal. Sam and Michiko repeated it.

Her father ate with steady concentration. The only sound in the room was the click of wooden chopsticks against their bowls, until Hiro's face twisted when his father offered him a fish eye and they all burst into laughter.

Chapter 9

JAP GIRL

The morning air was crisp but not cold — a perfect fall day. The breeze that brushed Michiko's hair brought the smells of damp earth, wet grass, and fading flowers. She gathered her coat tightly to her neck as she walked to the top of the lane for the school bus. At least she didn't have to walk all the way; a real school bus picked her up, not an old truck with benches in the back.

Tall and slim, like a gladiola stalk, Michiko often stared in the bathroom window wondering when she was going to produce buds. Everything she owned was too small. Even the sleeves of her coat were halfway up her arms. She wished she had a white wool coat like the one Mary wore to school. Michiko loved the way the large pleat at the back swung when Mary walked.

"Thank goodness for my sewing machine," her mother had said that morning with a deep sigh. "Everything will have to be adjusted."

Michiko knew what her mother really meant. No new clothes to anticipate. And there was no use going through the Eaton's catalogue talking about all the clothes she'd like to order, the way she used to do with Aunt Sadie. Her mother had no time to listen.

At breakfast, Michiko had watched her father as he looked through the newspaper before heading out into the fields, to see if he was still angry. *It was so unfair,* she thought. One of Hiro's favourite games was holding onto a tree branch, pulling his legs up and flipping over the branch. Her father had caught her playing this game in her skirt and sent her to her room to think about behaving like a lady.

Seeing a windfall, she picked up the apple and pitched it into the orchard. It soared across the grass and hit the gnarled trunk of an old apple tree. What she wouldn't give to have a pair of overalls like the ones Clarence wore, but girls around here didn't even wear slacks to school, let alone farm clothes. Overalls and running shoes were the two things she wanted more than anything else in the world.

Michiko pulled her new Hilroy exercise book to her chest for warmth. The cover had a drawing of a German plane crashing into the sea. In the drawing, the pilot was escaping by parachute, but the boys in her class filled their notebook covers with drawings of planes shooting at him, with drops of blood dripping to an ocean full of sharks.

Annie waved to her from the bus window as it pulled up. Today she wore a knitted cone-shaped hat with a red pom-pom on the top. Michiko knew the little girl would leave her seat to sit beside her, as she did every day.

"Do you like my hat?" was the first thing Annie asked. "My mom made it."

Michiko nodded.

"She could make you one too," Annie continued. "Then we could pretend to be twins."

Michiko smiled at the little girl's silly thought.

Annie glanced at the small drawstring bag that Michiko carried. "What's in the bag?"

"Gym clothes," Michiko said. She realized that even the longest of answers wouldn't stop Annie's inquisitiveness, so she kept them short.

Michiko had been surprised when Miss Barnhart told her to write *gym outfit* on her list. Her mother wasn't, however, and the next day she came home from school to find a navy blue jumper with a bib top, large pleated skirt, and matching bloomers on her bed. *A dress for physical education?* Michiko wondered. "What about running shoes?" she asked in a voice full of hope.

"They weren't on the list," her mother replied. "Besides, winter boots come first."

"But I can't do gym in my saddle shoes," Michiko complained. "They're too hard."

Eiko thought for a moment. "Then take those with you."

Michiko looked down at her battered corduroy house shoes. The rubber soles curled in at the edges, and there was a worn spot over each toe. "You want me to wear my slippers at school?" she shrieked. She threw herself face down onto her bed and covered her head with a pillow.

Eiko frowned and put her hands on her hips. "There are far more important things to spend money on in this world," she said as she left the room.

Michiko turned to the wall and sighed. If she wore slippers for gym, Carolyn Leahey would never stop making fun of her. *She's just like George King,* Michiko realized when her mother left. He had made her life miserable in her old town, and Carolyn was doing the same here.

"Billy is going to join the chess club," Annie said, bringing her back to reality. "He told my dad he's going to learn how to beat him. What about you?"

Annie's question set Michiko thinking. She'd completely forgotten about Sign-Up Day. The school offered special clubs in the winter months, and once a week classes would be dismissed early for extracurricular activities. Because of the war, daylight savings time was observed all year long. Town students needed written permission to walk home or had to be picked up. Carolyn made a big production of offering anyone a ride home in her father's old car. She never stopped bragging about their new convertible that would arrive in the summer. She claimed her father had chosen the green colour to match her eyes.

Michiko was just going to have to stay out of Carolyn's way as much as possible, and that meant making sure they were not in the same club. Then she had an idea.

"Annie," she said as they got off the bus, "would you like to do me a favour?"

"Sure," the little girl said, her eyes lighting up as she broke into a wide smile.

"Do you know a girl named Carolyn in my class?"

"Carolyn the Creep?" Annie rolled her eyes. "Billy complains about her all the time."

"Would you find out what club she's going to join and let me know at afternoon recess?"

Annie nodded and dashed across the playground to get in line.

"Don't forget to put your name on the club lists before you leave," Miss Barnhart reminded the class at dismissal. "The sheets are on the bulletin board outside the office."

Michiko followed the line of students down the hall. *Anything but choir,* she told herself as she stared at the labelled sheets of paper before her.

Checkers, Chess, Choir, Cooking, Junior Horticultural, Indoor Sports, Junior Farmers, Knitting, Pen Pals, Sewing, and Stamp Collecting were the choices. *These choices aren't that much fun,* she thought. In their Japanese clubs they had learned origami, which was how she knew to make paper flowers. Some kids, like her friend Kiko, learned *taiko*. Her aunt taught *odori*. Michiko looked up and down the lists again.

"Hurry up," someone called out from the back, "I ain't got all day."

"Yeah," Carolyn's shrill voice rose above the others. "Hurry up, Jap Girl."

Michiko froze, holding her pencil in midair.

"She's Japanese?" someone asked. "I thought she was Chinese."

"Aren't we fighting the Japs?" someone else asked.

"You're not kidding," a boy said. "Kamikazes sank a carrier in the Pacific last week."

"What's a kamikaze?" another boy asked.

"Why don't you ask her?" Carolyn suggested. "They're *her* people."

"What?"

Several students moved forward to hear better.

"Hey," someone cried out. "Quit pushing."

"Settle down," one of the teachers called out as he came out of the office. "Form a line and take turns, like good citizens."

Michiko could hardly see the paper in front of her when she signed her name. As she made her way to the bus, all she could think was, *Not again, not here too.*

"Mr. Takahashi and Dad spoke Japanese," Michiko said that night while doing the dishes. "But I didn't understand most of it."

Eiko turned a plate over to examine its cleanliness.

"What is *jidosha* and *yakyu*?" Michiko asked.

"*Jidosha* means car," her mother replied, "and *yakyu* means baseball. You should know those words by now," she said. "That's all your father ever talks about, cars and baseball."

"There was another word," Michiko said, working to keep her voice even. "What does kamikaze mean?"

Her mother put the dish on the table and looked at Michiko with a furrowed brow.

"Kamikaze," she repeated. "That's really two words. *Kami* is the word for god or divine spirit, and *kaze* means wind." Eiko shook her head. "What on earth could they be discussing?"

"Probably just someone's pitching style," Michiko said, skipping off to her room. She closed the door and sat at the end of her bed. *Those Japanese pilots must come out of the sky like lightning,* she thought. She picked up one of her slippers and threw it across the room. *Being Japanese is wrecking my whole life.*

The next morning, Michiko sat with her head in her hands at the breakfast table. Her mother placed a bowl of rice in front of her. She looked up and pushed it away. "Why can't we drink orange juice and eat cereal like everyone else?"

"How do you know everyone else eats cereal?"

How could she possibly explain her constant embarrassment during morning health inspection? Carolyn, this week's inspector, took her job of checking for clean fingernails, a handkerchief, and a good breakfast very seriously. Instead of asking, "Did you have a good breakfast?" Carolyn demanded to know what everyone ate and mocked their responses. She loved it when Michiko responded by saying "Rice."

"Rice?" Carolyn would repeat in a loud voice, feigning utter amazement. "You had rice for breakfast?"

"I am the only one in my class who has rice for breakfast," Michiko said to her mother.

"Well," her mother said, "it's your father's favourite breakfast food."

"Well, it is not mine," Michiko said loudly as she shoved the bowl across the table. "He can have two helpings from now on."

Chapter 10

ESCAPE

The gladioli fields were now just row upon row of twisted brown spikes. Michiko's father had told her bulbs couldn't be left in the ground over the winter. After digging them out, he and Mr. Palumbo would braid the leaves and hang them in the barn.

Michiko's shiny dark pigtails swung back and forth across the wide blue straps of her new overalls as she walked to the village to buy stamps. She had hoped she would finally get to live in a city of tall buildings and department stores, but all the village had to offer was a hardware store, drug store, grocery store, and school. It was no different than the ghost town.

Allen's Pharmacy had both Canadian and American flags in the window. Inside, Michiko spotted the familiar things from their drugstore: tooth paste, soap, talcum powder, and red rubber hot water bottles. She grimaced at the large bottles of cod liver oil but noticed they sold giant chocolate bars and big bags of popcorn already popped. They had greeting cards, wrapping paper, and something called hair spray. There was even a cooler full of popsicles and little cardboard cups of ice cream. When the brass bell above the shop door tinkled, Michiko remembered how much she liked the friendly chatter of their customers at her father's drug store, with all their bits and pieces of news.

She stood in line reading the handwritten signs posted on the cash register. *Bed Sitting Room $30.00* made her think how good it would be to have her aunt and uncle rent it.

"Hello, Millie." A familiar, unwelcome voice broke into her thoughts.

Michiko pretended not to hear Carolyn, even though she could feel the girl's warm breath on her neck. She moved her gaze to the ground, noticing the spotless white toes of the girl's majorette boots. Her own brown leatherwork boots, even though they were brand new, felt out of place beside those snub-nosed boots with their perfect tassels.

"I said *hello*," Carolyn said, with a nudge of her elbow. Her voice was friendly, as if there wouldn't be a confrontation, but Michiko knew it wouldn't last. She'd learned that much from George King. "I guess your thoughts are elsewhere," Carolyn said with a smile. "I suppose your father is away fighting with the rest of the soldiers."

Michiko felt her face grow hot as the person in front of her turned to look.

"Is he fighting for Japan or Canada?" Carolyn asked. "Remind me, what side is he on?"

Michiko took a breath and faced the girl. "My father has no side."

"What do you mean he has no side?" Carolyn said in a voice she made loud enough for all customers in the store to hear. "Everyone has to take a side when there is fighting."

There were nods from the people who stood around listening.

"He should be off fighting," Carolyn said. "Everyone else is."

Michiko's throat tightened as she moved forward in line.

Billy stepped out from one of the aisles. "That's not true, Carolyn," he said. "Someone has to stay home for the country."

Carolyn turned her back on him and continued. "So if your father didn't go off to war, what exactly did he stay home to do ..." she paused, looked at Billy and said, "... for the country?"

Michiko felt like a tadpole in a glass jar. She turned to Carolyn and took a deep breath. "My dad built roads," she blurted out.

"How do you build a road?" Carolyn let out a large, horse-like snort. "A road isn't made out of wood and bricks, like a house."

"He had to use dynamite to blast through the mountains," Michiko said in a voice she hoped was as loud as Carolyn's.

"Wow," Billy said. "I didn't know that. That's just as dangerous as being in the war."

Carolyn gave the boy a look of disdain. "I think your father went to work in the mountains just to avoid getting killed, like all the really, really, brave men." She made it sound as if getting killed was the only way to prove bravery.

"And what is *your* father doing, Carolyn?" Billy asked. "Is he out fighting?"

Carolyn turned on her heel and marched out the door.

Billy took Michiko by the elbow and led her away from the counter after she'd paid for her stamps. "They don't call her Carolyn the Creep for nothing."

Michiko nodded. "I guess your dad didn't go to war either."

"My dad," Billy replied, "says it makes him mad listening to all the talk about the men overseas doing their part. He's doing his part, too, but no one seems to think that way."

Michiko left the drugstore aware of the contemptuous stares from Carolyn and her girlfriends standing across the street. Carolyn pried the cardboard lid from her ice cream cup, licked it, and tossed it on the ground. She said something to her friends before she dug in with her wooden spoon, and they all laughed.

Michiko decided she would wait on a bench in the harbour until they left rather than attempt to walk past them. As she approached the parking lot, she spotted Naggie lounging in front of his grocery truck. She sat down amid the smell of the fishing boats tied up at the pier and listened to the slap of the waves. The breeze ruffled her hair as the seagulls engaged in their own arguments overhead.

But instead of leaving, Carolyn and the girls moved toward her.

The down on the back of Michiko's neck rose. She walked to the back of Naggie's truck and peeked around to see if they were really heading her way.

"Hey, Millie," Carolyn's voice called out as they approached. "You visiting Chinky-Chinky-Chinaman?"

Michiko mounted the steps, went inside the truck, and held her breath.

Carolyn strode across the parking lot and called out, "Hey, Millie, where are you? I want to tell you something."

No, you don't, Michiko thought. *You want to make fun of me, like you always do, and you probably want to pinch me.* The marks on her arm after their last confrontation at school had only just gone away. She pulled her ball cap from the back pocket of her overalls, stuffed her braids underneath, and crouched beside the stack of rice bags at the back. All she had to do was sit and wait for them to go away.

The girls moved along the gravel lot to the side of the truck.

"What you girls want to buy?" Naggie asked them as he followed them to the back.

"Nothing from you," Carolyn snapped. There was a burst of giggles from the other girls. "We're looking for someone."

"No one here but me," Naggie said. He lifted his set of steps and placed them inside.

Just go away, Michiko thought as Naggie shut the door. She waited a few more minutes to make sure they had gone and stood to leave, but Naggie had started the engine. The shelves shook, the goods rattled, and the truck lurched forward.

Michiko fell backward onto a sack of rice. She picked herself up, but the truck turned a corner and she fell sideways. She scrambled to her feet and grabbed on to the wooden shelves to steady herself as the truck picked up speed. *This can't be happening.* Michiko knew she had to get the truck to stop before it went too far, but how? She looked about in desperation.

Holding on to the shelves for support, Michiko reached for a bucket and an iron skillet. She made her way to the small counter Naggie used for weighing and packing. Bracing herself against the counter, she pounded them together. The truck slowed down for a moment.

Michiko waited.

The truck sped up.

This time Michiko pounded the bucket and stomped her feet.

The truck slowed down and swerved to one side. Michiko prayed Naggie was pulling over, but she didn't dare wait for the truck to come to a complete stop. If he found her in the back, he would turn around and drive her home. That would end in trouble. She would have to make a jump for it before he got out of the cab. She stumbled toward the door.

Her kick broke the rickety latch and the door swung open with a bang. Michiko watched the road move away from her, the grassy lawns to each side a blur. Taking a deep breath, she moved on to the rickety tail-gate, clinging to the other door. She could feel the truck slowing down. *Now or never,* she thought as the truck came to a rolling stop.

Michiko leapt to the side of the road, stumbled, and fell. She picked herself up, ran to a large, thick tree and hid behind it. It seemed to take forever before the engine started up again, but she dared not look until she heard it moving down the road, its wooden door tied with a long piece of frayed rope.

She brushed the gravel from her hands and the knees of her brand new overalls. Wherever she was, she had a long trudge ahead of her. All she had to do was figure out which way to go.

The chestnut tree Michiko hid behind was one of many that formed a huge avenue of trees on either side of a long drive. She walked until she came to a high, ornamental, wrought-iron fence. The gate, with a pattern of leaves, branches, and apples, stood open. The perfect green lawns before her were empty, except for a solitary robin bouncing through the grass. Michiko watched him cock his head to one side and fix his bright yellow eye on her.

"I know," she said to the bird, "it was a stupid thing to do."

She made her way across the lawn toward the large stone building that sat well back from the road in the middle of sprawling green grounds. This huge Victorian building, with brick turrets and gables, had tall windows tucked tightly into the stone walls. Like a place one would read about in a storybook, it gave her a fairy tale sense of doom.

Beside the steps, someone was pruning the bushes. The young man in a white T-shirt and blue jeans looked up from his gardening in surprise. He locked his shears and pushed back his baseball cap to watch her approach. A shock of blond hair fell across eyes the colour of a summer sky.

"I know this is private property," Michiko said to him. "I just need to know where I am."

"How can you not know where you are?" he asked with a small smile as he pushed back his hair and straightened his hat.

"Umm," Michiko said. "A friend dropped me off, but I guess at the wrong place."

"You don't know this place?" The young man extended his arms, seeming to have difficulty believing she actually didn't know where she was.

Michiko shook her head. An enormous feeling of fear brimmed up inside her, and she didn't want to speak.

"Well," he said, with a shrug, "you're on the grounds of Applegate School, the finest boys school in all of Canada."

"Oh," was all Michiko could say, because this information still didn't give her any idea as to how she was going to find her way home.

"Where were you headed?" the boy asked.

"Bronte Village," Michiko said.

He opened his shears, preparing to return to work. "You've got a bit of a walk ahead of you," he said as he snipped a dead branch from a bush. "Are you outside of the village or in the village itself?"

"Off the highway, just before the village."

"And you're going to walk?"

Michiko shrugged. *What else can I do?* Then she remembered the change in her pocket. "I'll just catch the bus," she said, trying to sound as if she knew what she was doing.

"The bus?" the boy said with a laugh. "With this shortage of gasoline, you could wait up to two hours. And if you get on, you'd have to stand for at least half an hour." He shook his head from side to side. Then he looked at his watch. "If you want to wait a few minutes, you can catch a ride with me."

Michiko pawed the grass with the toe of her boot. Her mother had told her again and again, *Never accept a ride with strangers.* She didn't know what to do.

"What's your name?" the boy asked.

What is my name? Michiko asked herself. *Who knows? Do I say Michiko or Millie?*

"Mich—" she started to say as the horn of a truck sounded at the side of the road. Two men in a pickup truck waited at the gates.

"Well, Mitch," the boy said, "my name is Eddie. If you don't mind sitting in the back of a truck, we can give you a lift."

Michiko watched as he wheeled a lawnmower up to the pickup truck and lifted it into the back. "Are you coming or not?" he asked. "I got to get to ball practice."

"You mean baseball?" Michiko ran to the back of the truck.

"No other kind of ball," Eddie said, grabbing her hand to help her up. It was a new experience for her, touching the hand of an older boy, especially one this good-looking. She flushed at the sensation.

"Most of the boys in my grade are in army cadets," Eddie said. "But I made the Ontario Summer League. We practice behind Bronte School." He banged the side of the truck, and it started up. "You a baseball fan?"

Michiko nodded. "The radio at home was always on for the World Series."

"That was one showdown," he said. "Those Cardinals won over a hundred games."

"And the Browns only got one homer the whole series," she replied.

Eddie nodded. "Baseball would be a lot better if most of the players weren't overseas," he said. "Look out, Hitler, the Yanks are coming, along with the Indians, the Red Sox, and the Tigers," he yelled through cupped hands. He went quiet for a moment. "I hope Stan Musial doesn't enlist. Did you catch that two-run homer he clubbed?"

Michiko nodded with a grin. Her father had hopped around the kitchen like a chicken that day. She began to recognize the area and decided she better get off at Billy's farm. Even though *Hitch a ride to save gasoline* was written on the chalkboard at school, her parents wouldn't be pleased to see her hop off the back of a truck.

It would be best if no one found out.

Chapter 11

MAIL

Instead of putting her name on the list for the Knitting Club, Michiko had accidently signed up for the Pen Pal Club. Once a week, this small group of girls was to gather to write to the Canadian soldiers, sailors, and airmen overseas. She sat with the end of her pencil in her mouth listening to the teacher's instructions.

Miss McIntosh peered over top of the tiny wire glasses perched on the end of her nose and announced, "Mail from home boosts a serviceman's morale. Our letters must be full of cheerful news. We will start by composing a group letter. Everyone will then copy it and send it out as their introductory letter."

"Do we put on our name and address?" a girl asked.

"First name only," the teacher replied. "The mail will be sent to their headquarters and forwarded from there. They will use the address of the school to write back or your own if you wish."

"What about stamps?" someone else asked.

"We will provide them for you."

Michiko made her copy of the group-composed letter in her notebook.

"After receiving a response, you can write your own letters to better suit the sender," Miss McIntosh said as she handed out boxes of greeting cards and stationery. "What you don't finish today you can continue at home. Sign the Christmas card and enclose a copy of the letter in each." She handed Michiko a box. "Don't forget to bring the boxes back for parcels."

At home, Michiko finished wishing the seven servicemen on her list Merry Christmas and Happy New Year and enclosed a copy of the letter. She sealed the last card and then moved to her bedroom window.

In the house behind them, Mr. Palumbo sat at the table reading a letter with his small stump of a pipe clenched between his teeth. Mrs. Palumbo walked past the kitchen window in her floral apron and headscarf, waving her hands about her head. She talked a lot, but Michiko never understood a word she said.

"Did you get our mail yet?" her mother asked as she popped her head in the doorway. She switched on Michiko's desk lamp, moved to her side, and then glanced out Michiko's bedroom window. "That woman does nothing but complain," she said.

"How do you know?" Michiko asked. "She doesn't speak English."

"I can tell what she is saying by the way she uses her

hands and her eyes." Her mother pulled the curtains shut, giving the room a warm, dusky glow.

Michiko lifted her coat from the hook by the door. Outside, the smell of smoke from her father's bonfire drifted through the cold air. All the brown leaves of the gladioli bulbs had been removed and were now being burned. She had watched her father clean the corms with a little wooden brush. Michiko thought they looked like large, flat, hairy chestnuts lying in their long, thin boxes of sawdust. Hundreds and hundreds of bulbs would wait out the winter on their specially built shelves in Mr. Downey's barn.

Right now her father would be sitting at the long wooden table in the barn writing out the names of the different kinds of flowers in his private notebook. People expected him to know which kinds they were talking about when they called to place an order. With forty-seven and a half acres of flowers, there was a lot to remember. Sometimes he worked late into the night making small sketches and Japanese symbols next to bulbs with names like American Beauty, Friendship, and Snow Prince.

Her mother would often take him a hot drink and stay to help. But Michiko wasn't allowed. If she accidently knocked a bulb to the ground, it couldn't be sold.

Michiko walked along the dark laneway until she came to the mailbox that sat on a post of the wooden fence and pulled down the little metal door. Picking up the mail at the end of the lane was much better than visiting the musty old general store with its creaky wooden floors. Evening sounds were different as well. Living close to a main road, she now heard the screech of tires and once in a while the wail of a siren. Michiko missed the sounds of her previous home, the soothing gurgles of water rushing across the stones in the creek bed to the lake and the short sharp caws of the crows. It was hard to believe that at one time she had been afraid of the beautiful, haunting call of the loon. The howling wolves used to send chills down her spine as well, but she missed them, too.

Michiko pulled out the mail. There was nothing from Clarence. She decided to give up on the idea of him ever writing her a letter. There was nothing from Mrs. Morrison either. But Aunt Sadie's letter excited her. She couldn't wait to hear it. She rushed back to the house to hand it to her mother.

Dear Family,

I hope my letter finds you all well. I am sure the children are growing fast and it will be no time before little Hannah is walking. Michiko must write me about her new school.

Winter has settled in the mountains once again. Edna and Ralph have brought out their sleigh for moving about in the snow. She looks so royal sitting up front in her new fur hat.

I found out that the Sakamoto family is now living in Toronto. Ed, who used to work in a bank, was only able to get a job at Eaton's stocking shelves. Apparently there is a terrific shortage of workers for non-essential industries. I believe there are so many places that Kaz could fit into, if he would rid himself of the idea of donning a uniform. But he hasn't, in fact ...

Eiko paused in her reading. Michiko watched her mother's eyes move back and forth across the tightly-written lines before she said, "Sam, listen."

... he found out the Canadian Army Japanese Language School is seeking candidates. The RCMP gave a man in Slocan clearance and a permit to leave.

Michiko's father put down the work boot that he was cleaning.

No sooner does Edna's husband come home than mine packs to leave. That's right. Kaz got his wish and will soon be in uniform.

"What team is he on?" Michiko asked as she wiped little Hannah's mouth.

Sam and Eiko looked at their daughter in surprise.

"Team," Eiko repeated. "What do you mean team?"

"What baseball team signed him up?" Michiko asked. "What's his uniform?"

Eiko looked at Sam. He shrugged as if to give her permission to explain.

"Kaz joined the army," Eiko said quietly, then went back to the letter.

He sees it an act of faith, as if donning a uniform was a pledge to be a loyal Canadian.

Michiko thought about the boys who came to school to show off their cadet jackets with the word CANADA on the shoulder. Then her face took on a puzzled look. "Is Uncle Kaz going to fight in the war?"

"Yes," Sam replied.

"Why?"

"Why not?"

"Because he is Japanese."

"He is Japanese-Canadian," Sam said. "It's no different from being Italian-Canadian, like the Palumbos."

Michiko thought about Mrs. Morrison's husband. His ship was attacked, and he was lost at sea before she learned he was safe. "It could be dangerous for him," she said, looking down at her feet, "like the other soldiers."

Sam lifted his other boot from the newspaper covering the kitchen table and gave it a quick brush. "Your Uncle Ted tried to sign up with the Canadian navy," he said.

"He did?"

"They wouldn't take him," he said. "That's why he took the job building houses."

"Did you ever want to wear a uniform?" Michiko asked.

Sam spat on his boot and kept on cleaning.

He's not going to answer my question. Michiko rose from the table to head for her room.

Sam put down his boot as the colour drained from his face. When he spoke, his voice was thin, and it quavered. "I have lived and worked in Canada longer than I did in Japan. They still don't see me as a Canadian because of my face." He looked down.

Eiko put her hand on his arm.

Sam lifted his head and cleared his throat to make his voice sound strong again. "But we need to put all these things behind us now," he said. "We can spend the rest of our lives blaming the war, the government, the camp, the prime minister. Instead of complaining, we should work hard to make things better."

"Things will be better when it's baseball season," Michiko said, trying to cheer him up.

Sam gave her a wide smile. "Like the games in the ghost town," he said. "Everyone stopped looking at the colour of other people's skin and started looking at their batting average."

Michiko had one Christmas card left. She decided to send it to her Uncle Kaz. Mrs. McIntosh would know how to get it to him.

Christmas preparations brought a small tree that filled their little house with the scent of pine. To Michiko's and Hiro's delight, their mother purchased lights and a box of tinsel.

"When I was little," she told them, as they decorated, "the pine tree stood outside the house, near the front door."

Michiko looked at her in surprise.

"Your Uncle Ted used to go with Geechan to the woods to cut it down." She inhaled the scent of pine and smiled. "Your grandfather would always say, 'If the pine tree is strong and always green, our house will be blessed with strength and long life.'" Eiko turned to Michiko with a broad smile. "Sadie was the one who insisted the tree be set up indoors, like those of the rest of the children in her class."

Christmas morning, Michiko was thrilled with the books from her parents. Aunt Sadie had sent them a game of Snakes and Ladders. Uncle Ted made Hiro Noah's ark, complete with four pairs of animals. The tiny red rowboat and set of oars was for her. Mrs. Morrison put a whole dollar bill in their Christmas card just for Michiko.

That afternoon, Mrs. Palumbo left a covered casserole dish on their kitchen table. Eiko lifted the lid to reveal a large square of cheese and tomato sauce.

"What is it?" Michiko asked as she sniffed at the steaming dish.

"Tonight's dinner," her mother responded, as she placed Mrs. Palumbo's masterpiece into the oven. "Mr. Palumbo told your father she would be sending it over."

Christmas night, the Minagawa family gathered at the kitchen table, anxious to try the dish that filled the house with its spicy aroma. The strange food didn't give Michiko the usual feeling of happiness as she unfolded her napkin. Her father's hand shook as he accepted a plate of this unfamiliar dish the Palumbo family called lasagna. But to everyone's surprise, the frilly noodles, the delicious savoury meat, tomato sauce, and sharp cheese blended together perfectly.

There were other treats as well. Mr. Downey had given their family a fancy wrapped box. When Eiko lifted the lid and opened the wax paper, she discovered a cake of dried fruit and nuts, topped with white icing and glazed cherries. She served it with dishes of red Jello.

But the feast they were all waiting for was New Year's dinner, the biggest holiday of the year for the Japanese. Eiko had cooked from dawn, preparing thick rolls of *nori*-wrapped rice stuffed with strips of omelette and mushrooms. There was *chawanmushi* and chicken *yakitori*, too.

Mr. Takahashi arrived in a dark suit, which was much too big for him and made him look thinner than usual. His wife's red woollen coat covered her from shoulders to ankles. Her dark hair, sitting in a pile on top of her peony-pink face, gave her the look of a fat little robin.

Mrs. Takahashi's floral dress seemed so vivid against her mother's white tablecloth that Michiko couldn't help but think about the beautiful dresses her Aunt Sadie once owned.

"How are your studies?" Mrs. Takahashi asked as her husband moved away from the table, in deep discussion with her father. Nothing seemed to escape her attention, and she asked a lot of questions. *Almost nosy,* Michiko thought.

"Fine," Michiko answered, but seeing her mother's direct stare, she added, "I get As."

The woman smiled. "And your studies at home?" she asked as Michiko's mother rose to take Hiro to bed.

"I do all my homework," Michiko answered.

"I mean your Japanese studies," the little woman said as she smoothed her napkin over her skirt.

Michiko did not know how to answer. Speaking Japanese had been forbidden in the ghost town. Other than the *Kairanban*, their camp newspaper, no one even dared to write Japanese in public. "I haven't ..." Michiko began.

Mrs. Takahashi reached out and patted Michiko's arm. "These days one can't exactly walk into a store and ask for Japanese books," she said.

Michiko nodded and gave a small sigh, pretending it mattered.

"But there must be something you can learn from," Mrs. Takahashi continued. "Does your mother not have any letters written in Japanese? Something you could use for practice."

"I have some old letters of my grandfather's," Michiko said. "But how can I practice if I don't know what they say?"

Hiro raced past them, avoiding his mother's attempt to put him to bed.

"Your mother has her hands full," Mrs. Takahashi announced. "Give me the letters. I will translate them." She shook a small, fat finger in Michiko's face. "Do not forget your heritage, and never believe the country of your father's birth is as evil as everyone is saying."

Michiko excused herself and went to her room. She opened Clarence's little blue box and removed the packet of thin blue papers. Then she reached across her desk to her jam jar of paper flowers and chose the paper iris.

When her mother arrived in the living room carrying a tray of teacups, Mrs. Takahashi raised the flower to her nose. "It looks real enough to have perfume," she said. "Thank you."

The smile on her mother's face told Michiko she approved of the gesture.

That night, Michiko listened to the gentle murmur of conversation and laughter that came from the living room. As the teacups clinked, Michiko thought how easy it seemed to be for adults to make friends.

Chapter 12

SNOWSTORM

The pale light that filled her bedroom told Michiko there was no hurry to get up for the school bus. The heavy snow the weatherman promised had fallen. She pushed her feet into her slippers, wrapped her *hant-en* around her, and pulled back the curtains. Michiko pressed her hand against the windowpane to clear a spot through the ferns of frost. Snow sculpted the wooden tri-pods of the pole beans into soft cones and turned the rest of the abandoned garden into strange shapes. The gladioli fields looked like blocks of tofu. She could see the gnarled branches of the black apple trees clearly against the white.

"Schools are closed," her mother said as she put her head around the door. "I heard it on the radio. With you here minding Hiro, I'll be able to get a lot done at the big house."

Michiko sat back down on her bed. *Of course, I will have to look after my little brother. Why did I think I would have a whole day to do what I wanted?*

Her father sat at the kitchen table cradling a cup of coffee, which was unusual. Most mornings he was long gone by the time she rose. Michiko reached for a bowl and took it over to the pot of oatmeal that waited on the stove. The thought of no school brought a small sense of relief. She was tired of moving about the building like an invisible person. At least back at the Hardware Store School she had friends to invite home. She had been at Bronte Creek Public School for six months and still had no one she could really call a friend.

Hiro appeared, clutching his kitten. Michiko placed the oatmeal on the table for him and reached for another bowl.

Back in September, Michiko had told herself that friends weren't that important because she had her family, coloured pencils and a sketch pad, and a whole library of books in town, but on a day like today, with all this snow, all she could think of was sliding down the mountain on empty rice bags with Kiko and the snowball fights she and Clarence had with George.

Michiko wanted to get to know the girl she sat beside much better. Michiko liked Mary's polite ways and neat appearance. She had a perfect cupid's-bow mouth, straight white teeth, a small snub nose, and bouncy curls. Mary wasn't perfect in every way, because she was a bit of a scatterbrain, always losing or forgetting things. Most times when the teacher was talking, she was staring off into space. But Carolyn Leahey seemed to be in charge of who made friends with whom in her class, and she had made it clear to all the girls right from the first day that Michiko was to be ignored.

"Did you sleep well?" her father asked.

Michiko nodded.

"I went out like a lightning!" he said, making Michiko smile at his English, like whenever he referred to his "cold feets."

She placed her bowl in front of her. Then she planted her elbows on either side, settled her face in her hands, and released a great sigh.

"What's the matter?" Her father tilted his head to contemplate her.

"Nothing," she said. There was no point in telling him how Dorothy winced and waved her hand in front of her nose as if Michiko's odour was too much to bear, or Sharon knocked Michiko's books off her desk. Once, while glaring at her, Carolyn had jabbed the point of her compass into Michiko's new dictionary, making a hole. That gesture was meant to be a threat.

It wasn't any better on the playground, either. A large girl named Leslie loved to yell "Mount Fuji!" and dump snow down the back of her neck.

Her father would only tell her to ignore it, which she tried to do, but it was getting harder and harder every day. Yesterday she'd found a cartoon drawing of a slant-eyed person with large buck teeth inside her desk.

"Everything okay at school?" he asked. He glanced at the calendar posted on the kitchen wall, where REPORT CARD DAY was written. "You gonna get good marks?"

Michiko nodded as she lifted her spoon to her mouth.

Eiko appeared in the kitchen, carrying Hannah. "The snow's supposed to stop by noon," she said, sitting to dress the baby in her woollen clothes. "Have you shovelled a path?"

"Few minutes," her father said, pulling his coat from the hook by the door. Mr. Palumbo, in his black beret and huge sheepskin coat, was already clearing the snow from his front walk.

After breakfast, Michiko washed their bowls and sat down at the table with her sketchpad. With a few quick strokes she drew the shape of her brother's head, his short cap of hair, and small nose as he looked out the window. Her father cleared the lane with a plough attached to the farm truck. The great piles of snow reminded her of the British Columbia mountains. Michiko stuffed her triple-socked feet into her black boots with their huge teeth-like treads. She would show Hiro how to make a snowman.

Mr. Palumbo crossed the yard just as she was attempting to place the head on top of the other two giant snowballs. With a smile, he took the oddly shaped ball of snow from her arms and positioned it on top. Then he doffed his hat to the sculpture and said, "*Buon giorno.*"

Michiko giggled. "How do you say *thank you* in Italian?"

"*Grazie,*" he replied with a grin that made his big round eyes look doggy.

"*Grazie,*" Michiko repeated with a smile.

She and Hiro found sticks for the arms in the woodpile and wizened apples in the shed for the snowman's face. A large stalk of undersized Brussels sprouts stuck out of the compost heap. Michiko gave it a great tug. Brussels sprout buttons would be perfect. By the time they finished, the snow had stopped falling, red streaks had appeared in the sky, and miso soup waited for them on the stove.

Michiko picked Hannah up from her pink blanket on the floor of the living room. "Come and see our new family friend," she said. She took her sister to the window to wave at the snowman. *Too bad we can't keep him,* Michiko thought. *But just like all the other friends in my life, he won't last.*

The next day, although it was cold, the roads and schools were open.

"You should all be very proud of yourselves," Mrs. McIntosh said as she passed out the first batch of letters addressed to the Pen Pal Club. "By the look of this pile of correspondence, the boys overseas were more than happy to hear from you." She stopped in front of Michiko and smiled. "You did especially well," she said, placing three envelopes on the desk.

One envelope was addressed in large, loopy letters that reminded her of a circus. Another had tall, thin letters that leaned like grass in the wind. The third's writing was small and sloppy, with blobs of ink. She couldn't decide which one to open first, feeling that she would somehow slight the other two with her choice. She picked them up, made a fan, and turned to the girl beside her. "Pick one for me," she said. The girl looked about the room as if to seek approval, shrugged, and pulled an envelope.

Dear Millie, the letter began, only the letters were so thin and tight together, it could have been Molly or Maggie.

> *I received your letter last week. How kind of you to write to me. This far away from home you sometimes get the feeling everyone has forgotten about you. I can hardly remember when we weren't at war. All last week we had blackened faces and hands as we did night patrols. Every time the moon came out from behind the clouds, the sergeant hissed, "Face down," and we lay along the brow of a hill. Some guys ended up lying down in the rocky bed of a stream. We had to stay there for some time waiting for cloud cover, and a couple of the guys fell asleep. They got into trouble for that, I can tell you. The patrols paid off, though, because we are moving camp in the morning.*
>
> *Know anything about baseball? Is it true the St. Louis Browns have a one-armed man on the team? See if you can find out his name, if it's true. The news is so old and mixed up by the time it gets to us, one never knows if it's a joke or not.*
>
> *I look forward to hearing from you again.*
>
> *Gerald*

Michiko folded the letter along its crease and slipped it back into the envelope. She hadn't heard about the one-armed baseball player, but she knew who to ask. She decided to read them all before answering and opened another envelope. Large, loopy writing filled the pages.

Dear Millie,

I received your letter last week. I'd heard of soldiers receiving letters from strange girls but didn't think I'd get one. The Red Cross said to put our name down, and so I did.

I just got back from having my first haircut and bath in six weeks. We had been camped out in a house that had no windows or roof, which isn't pleasant when it rains. One good thing is that it was out of artillery range, so at least a guy could sleep straight through when not on night patrol. We are not allowed to tell you where we are.

I got a roll of newspapers with this letter and some of the guys are mad at the way the reporters keep saying it's almost over. They shouldn't be telling that to our side, they should be telling the Jerries. One headline said the enemy is short of guns, but if you were here you'd know that wasn't true. Once this show ends, I guess we will be giving it to the Japs.

Michiko gave out a small gasp but read on. *Send me your picture so I can show the guys.*

Your army buddy, Johnny

Michiko gave a wry smile at the last line. *Send him my picture?* She could just imagine what Johnny and his friends would say to a picture of a Japanese girl, but that didn't matter anyway because she didn't have one. Cameras in the hands of Japanese people had been forbidden for years. Mrs. Morrison had taken the last picture of her family at Sadie's wedding, and if she even had a copy of that photograph, it would mean sending this soldier a whole family of "Japs." She shivered at the thought of his reaction. Michiko refolded the letter, put it in its envelope, and reached for the last one.

This envelope was spattered with blobs of ink.

Dear Millie,

The ink blot after the comma was huge. The writer drew an arrow from it to the next line.

> *This pen is lousy, so please excuse the scratchings and ink blotches. My fountain pen is somewhere at the bottom of the English Channel. This was all that the Red Cross had to offer. So I am stuck.*
>
> *Is rationing serious in Canada? I haven't seen a steak for months. Clothing is scarce as well, which is why we spend so much time in uniform. Some guys even get married in them.*
>
> *I don't have a lot to say, but you can write and ask me questions. Don't ask about where I am, though. Even if I try to tell you, the censors will block it out.*
>
> *Francis*

Michiko picked up the fountain pen with the name and phone number of the gladioli farm that sat in the little trough at the top of her desk. Mr. Downey gave them to his customers. Surely he could spare one for a soldier.

"Do you have an extra pencil?" Mary whispered to her the next morning. Her shiny, curly hair seemed to dance about the shoulders of her white angora sweater.

Michiko nodded. She handed one across the aisle and watched it clatter to the floor as Mary dropped it. Michiko picked it up and handed it to her again.

"Thanks," Mary said. "I forgot mine at home."

Mary didn't have her arithmetic book either and asked if she could share. Michiko pushed her desk over and opened her text.

"I usually forget to bring it home," Mary confessed. "Then I forget to bring it back."

Michiko shrugged.

"I'm staying for lunch today," Mary whispered, "because of the snow."

"You can eat with me," Michiko offered, trying not to sound too eager.

Mary gave a quick glace over her shoulder. She didn't have to say anything else. Carolyn had already made plans for her.

When Michiko entered the lunch room, the noise of scraping chairs and children talking told her a lot of students had decided not to push their way home through the drifts. Some sat on the floor with their backs to the wall.

"Over here," Annie called out as she waved from her brother's side. "I saved you a seat."

Across from them sat Carolyn, Sharon, and Mary.

Michiko plunked her library book on top of the table and her *furoshiki* on top.

"Look at that," Carolyn said, opening her pink tin lunchbox. "Millie's got a hobo sack."

Annie looked at the girl with flashing eyes. "It is not," she said. "It's a furshopiki!"

Michiko smiled at the little girl's mispronunciation.

"All you need is a stick, and you can carry it across your shoulder," Sharon said.

Michiko lifted her lunch bundle and shoved her library book to one side.

"What's this?" Carolyn asked, seeing the tip of a sheet of paper sticking out from between the pages. She extended a hand of badly painted fingernails.

Michiko pulled the book back just as Carolyn's fingers caught hold of the edge of the paper. She waved the folded paper about in front of her face. "Is it a love note?" Carolyn looked at Billy, who munched away on his sandwich. "Billy, are you putting love notes into Millie's library books?"

Annie looked at her brother in astonishment.

"Shut up, Carolyn," Billy said through a mouthful of bread and jam.

"Millie and Billy sitting in a tree," Carolyn chanted.

Sharon joined in, "K-I-S-S-I-N-G."

Mary took the paper from Carolyn, opened it, and gasped.

"Is it really a love note?" Sharon asked with glee.

"It's beautiful," Mary said, turning the paper for all to see. "Did you draw it?"

Carolyn leaned in. Her eyes went from the sketch to Michiko and back again with the unblinking attention of a hawk watching a mouse. "You copied it from a magazine," she said.

Michiko reached across the table and took the sketch back. "It's my little brother." She turned the paper for Annie to see. "He was watching the snow plough when I drew it."

Annie took the drawing and held it out for Billy to see.

"I've seen her little brother," Billy told Carolyn. "It looks just like him."

"Can I have it?" Annie asked.

Michiko shook her head, took the folded the paper, and put it back inside the book. "It's just a sketch," she said. "When I get some paints, I'm going to finish it."

"You should ask the teacher if you can work on it in art class," Mary said. "It's good."

"Too good," Carolyn said, packing up her half-eaten lunch. "She traced it."

Michiko's cheeks burned red, but she felt a tingle of excitement knowing Mary liked her drawing. If she could just find a way to spend time with her without Carolyn around. She opened her package of wax paper and removed a rice ball.

"Ugh," Carolyn said. "What are you eating?"

Michiko placed a tiny white ball rolled in sesame seeds in the palm of her hand for all to see.

"Get it away," Carolyn shouted as she shoved her metal lunch pail across the table.

Michiko's rice balls bounced and scattered across the floor, and her apple rolled under a chair.

"Oops," Carolyn said. "Gotta go." She leaped from the table. Sharon followed, and they both went out the door.

Michiko stared at what was left of her lunch sitting in her hand.

Annie retrieved the apple, blew on it, and placed

it in front of Michiko. "She did that on purpose," she said. "Carolyn's mean."

Mary lifted the wax paper that held the other half of her sandwich. "Here," she said, offering it to Michiko. "It's just peanut butter."

Not wanting to confess she had never tasted peanut butter, Michiko smiled and took it with thanks.

"Do you have to go straight home?" Michiko asked Mary at the end of the school day.

"French lessons on Monday, piano lessons on Tuesday, dance lessons on Wednesday, Four H Club on Thursday," Mary said, counting each out on a finger.

"Wow," was all Michiko could say.

"I gotta run," Mary said. "My piano teacher will be waiting."

Michiko glanced at her coat hook. "You forgot your scarf," she said, holding it out to her.

"Thanks," Mary said, turning back. "My mother says I'd forget my head if it wasn't fastened on." She wound the scarf about her neck.

Michiko turned back to her hanger to get her coat. On the shelf above Mary's hook sat a familiar brown envelope. She picked up Mary's report card and placed it on the teacher's desk. She couldn't imagine going home without her report card. Her parents would be so furious they'd make her walk all the way back to school to get it.

Chapter 13

STRAIGHT As

Michiko watched as her mother opened her report card. She knew she had As in Science, Arithmetic, Grammar, History, Geography, and Art. It was Physical Education she was worried about. Michiko's throat went dry as her mother studied the mark and the comments.

"*Michiko needs to better apply herself on the equipment,*" Eiko read out loud.

"What equipment?" her father asked. He put down the gardening manual he was studying. She couldn't help noticing how scratched and blistered his hands had become. Michiko looked down at her lap. At first she had been excited to see mats, parallel bars, and the balance beam. Miss Barnhart named each piece of equipment as an older student demonstrated how to use it. The long leather structure, she learned, was called a pommel horse. But every Friday, while the rest of the girls put on their canvas running shoes, Michiko had to remove her shoes and socks in order to participate. Not only was she cold, the wooden springboard was cracked in several places, and she was terrified of getting a splinter.

"What's wrong?" Mary asked the first time Michiko came to a sudden halt at the bottom of the board. "All you have to do is run up to it, bounce, and jump over. Watch."

Mary ran up to the board, bounced, and soared over the horse.

The rest of the girls took their turns.

Michiko willed herself to run across the gym floor, but the minute her bare feet touched the edge of the rough wood, she stopped.

"It won't bite you," Carolyn called out. "It's not a real horse."

"That's enough," Miss Barnhart called out, but not before the rest of the class laughed.

"Gymnastics equipment," Michiko said to her parents, coming out of her reverie. "Vaulting over a pommel horse is hard," she complained. "My body doesn't want to do it."

"Any grade below A is not acceptable," her mother said sternly. She put the report back into its envelope.

"If I had a pair of running shoes …" Michiko began, but her mother put up her hand.

"Shoes don't have magical properties," she said. "You need to make an effort, just as the teacher says. I expect a big improvement."

Mary was waiting for Michiko when she got off the school bus the next day. "I need to talk to you," she said, taking Michiko's arm. To her surprise, Mary led her across the playground to where Carolyn waited with Nancy.

"We can work at each other's houses after school," Carolyn was saying. On seeing Michiko approach, she lowered her schoolbooks and rolled her eyes. "She lives way out on some stupid farm, the very last stop on the bus route."

Billy's is the last stop, Michiko thought but didn't bother to correct her.

"We want you to work with us on our project," Mary said.

Carolyn shot Mary a look of annoyance.

Michiko's eyes widened with surprise. "You do?"

"You are an artist," Mary said, drawing her closer into the group. "Of course we want you. That's why we're asking before we get into class."

Michiko was still in a state of disbelief when they moved into the classroom. She had fully expected to be working on her own.

"There are three categories to choose from," Miss Barnhart explained, "legends, fairy tales, or tales from history." She wrote the titles across the chalkboard. "Each group must have at least one boy or girl."

The class groaned.

"You have the rest of the week to let me know who is in your group."

At lunch Michiko suggested Billy be part of their group.

"Billy?" Carolyn repeated loudly, making him look up from his comic book and stick out his tongue.

"See," she said, "he's so rude."

"But he lives close to me," Michiko said. "I could work with him at my house, while you work with Mary at hers. We can all meet on Saturday at the library."

"We have to have a boy," Mary reminded Carolyn.

Carolyn stared at Billy's yellow hair across the room. "It's bad enough seeing him Monday to Friday. I don't want to have to look at him on Saturday."

"I'll ask him," Michiko said as she rose from her seat.

Annie's face lit up when she approached.

"Billy," Michiko asked, "would you like to work on the project with me?"

Billy looked up from his comic book and shrugged.

"Say yes, Billy," Annie pleaded. "Millie can come to our house. Say yes."

"Okay, I guess," Billy said. "I haven't thought much about it."

That afternoon, Michiko waited at the bus stop, wiggling her toes inside her boots to keep them warm. Billy was throwing snowballs onto the road.

Carolyn and Mary walked by. "I'm going to ask Richard to join our group," Carolyn said. "He lives on our street."

"You can't," Mary replied. "You know Michiko asked Billy."

"She can have Billy," Carolyn said. "You and I can work with Richard and Nancy."

Mary stopped walking and said something.

"I don't care if she can draw or not," Carolyn yelled, stamping her foot in the snow. "I'm not going to work with a Jap girl."

Michiko climbed onto the bus with a heavy heart. Without Carolyn and Mary, it could leave her and Billy working on their own.

Oakville library, on the main street of town, had large picture windows, low tables with comfortable chairs, and walls and walls of books. Several groups of children from Mrs. Barnhart's class were gathered to work on their projects. As it turned out, Mary had stood up to Carolyn and agreed to come and meet with Michiko and Billy after her 4-H Club meeting. Her older brother was to meet her there to drive her home.

It wasn't easy deciding on the people they were going to research. Mary wanted to work on fairy tales so she could write about princesses, and Billy wanted legends so he could tell the story of Paul Bunyan. Betty, who had taken Carolyn's place, couldn't decide.

"If we do people from history," Michiko suggested, "Mary could do an Indian princess and Billy could find all kinds of heroes."

When Mary's brother, Eddie, walked into the library late Saturday afternoon, Michiko immediately recognized him as the boy who had given her a lift home from Applegate College. She pulled her book up over face and slid down in her seat.

He walked over to Billy and ruffled his hair. Billy looked up with a giant smile.

"How's the arm?" Eddie asked in a low voice.

Billy leapt to his feet to mimic winding up and making a pitch.

"Hey, sis," Eddie whispered to Mary as he pulled a paperback novel from his back pocket, "I'll just read until you're ready." He moved to a comfortable chair near the window.

Michiko lowered the book.

"My brother is so lucky," Mary said, putting her elbows on the table and her head in her hands. "He doesn't have to go to school in the springtime."

"What do you mean he doesn't have to go to school?" Michiko asked.

"The government thought up a plan to help out the farmers," Mary explained. "If you have straight As first and second term, you don't have to go to school for the third term. You can work on a farm. It's called being *expect* or something like that."

"Exempt?" Michiko asked. "Is that what you mean?"

"That's it," Mary said with a sigh. "All he has to do is find a farmer to sign his papers, and he works instead of going to school. He also gets a government certificate for a new bicycle, which is what he really wants."

"My dad might sign," Billy said. "Men are always quitting to work at the basket factory." He rubbed his head in thought. "I won't be playing any ball if we don't get help."

At least you get to play ball, Michiko thought. The boys had laughed loudly when she'd said she wanted to play.

Miss Barnhart handed out the project grades, giving each group a copy of her comments.

The four of them were very proud of their project, "Little Trails Through History." Mary's mother had typed out the stories, and Michiko had done a full-page watercolour for each. Betty had designed the covers with birch bark. Billy hole-punched the covers and the pages, protected them with reinforcements, and put the whole thing together with hinged metal rings.

"*Well chosen stories,*" Betty read out to them, "*excellent illustrations and fine presentation.* Miss Barnhart gave us an A!"

"We got an A?" Mary asked in disbelief.

Billy's eyes shone.

Betty nodded and turned to Michiko with a smile.

"This is absolutely amazing," Mary said, clapping her hands. "I have never had an A in anything in my entire life." She paused and thought for a moment. "I've never even had a B."

She closed her eyes and crossed her hands over her chest. "I'll bet I get a present."

"Wait until my father sees this. He won't believe it!" Billy said. "I'll get to play ball this summer for sure."

Betty folded the paper and handed it to Michiko. "Who wants to stand around in a field of dandelions waiting to get hit on the head?"

"My parents will be so grateful," Mary said, grabbing Michiko's arm as they went out onto the playground. "I always fail arithmetic, and I get Ds in science. They will not believe this!"

Michiko drew Mary over to the school wall. "I didn't know you failed arithmetic," she said in a low voice. No wonder Mary wasn't in a hurry to take home her report card.

"Didn't you know I was a dummy?" Mary said with a casual laugh. "That's why I get all those other lessons. If I'm not good at school, I gotta be good at something else."

"You are not a dummy," Michiko insisted. "You read ten times more stories than we did."

"I love to read," Mary said, "but I'm pretty dumb at everything else. That's why I go to this school instead of the other one."

"What other school?" Michiko asked.

"I used to go to a private school, you know, like Applegate, only mine was for girls."

"Why did you change?"

"I had to," Mary said, dragging Michiko away from the wall. "My dad refused to pay for a fancy school when my marks were so low." She shrugged. "The teachers were happy to see me leave."

"Do you want to make a deal?" Michiko asked Mary the next day at recess.

"What kind of deal?"

"I'll help you pass arithmetic if you help me with something."

"How can I help you?" Mary asked with a frown. "You're good at everything."

"Not physical education," Michiko confessed.

"But I can't stay after school," Mary said. "I've got my lessons."

"And I have to catch the bus," Michiko said, "but you can stay for lunch."

Mary smiled. "I'll ask," she said.

Michiko pulled her socks up tight and stepped into Mary's running shoes. She ran up to the springboard and gave a little bounce, but she had no idea what to do next.

Mary came to her side and placed Michiko's hands on the handles. "Put your hands like this after you jump. Just think, run, bounce, hands, legs. It will all come together." Mary turned to Miss Barnhart and said, "She needs to try again."

"And again, and again, and again," Carolyn said, for all to hear.

Miss Barnhart nodded. "Try again," she said with a tight smile.

Michiko took a deep breath. She imagined the pommel horse as one of the fences around the field. She just knew she could clear it this time. She ran hard, bounced hard, put her hands on the handles and lifted her legs. She landed with a splat on top of the horse.

"You got up in the air," Mary said, clapping her hands, "didn't she, Miss Barnhart?"

The teacher nodded. "Try again, Millie."

Some of the girls on the other equipment stopped to watch.

This time the whole class watched. Michiko cleared the horse and landed on her feet.

Miss Barnhart beamed. "Do it again," she said.

"Show-off," Carolyn called out. But to Michiko's surprise, the rest of the girls clapped.

At lunch, Mary stared out the window chewing her pencil as Michiko went over the arithmetic lesson Miss Barnhart had taught that morning. "I've been thinking," she said. "There is a much easier way for me to get good marks in arithmetic, without missing recess."

"Are you going do your homework every night?"

"I wasn't thinking of that," Mary said. "Carolyn gave me an idea."

Michiko's brow darkened. "What is it?" she asked.

"Well," Mary explained, "she said it was too late for me to study everything I ignored all term, and there was a much faster way."

Michiko waited to hear what this magical plan was. As far as she knew, the only way to get good marks was to study.

"We've got a test this Friday, right?"

Michiko nodded.

"Well," Mary said in a whisper, "since we sit right beside each other ... if maybe you could keep your paper close to the edge of your desk, if you know what I mean."

Michiko understood exactly what Carolyn wanted her to do. She flipped her arithmetic book closed, put her notebook on top of it, and her empty lunch bundle on top of that, and rose to leave. Her parents would disown her if they knew she'd let someone copy from her test paper.

"We won't get caught," Mary called out. "Carolyn says she does it all the time."

"We won't get caught because it won't happen," Michiko said quietly. She walked out of the room, worrying. *If I don't let Mary copy, will we still be friends?*

Chapter 14

TWO LETTERS

Michiko opened her window one morning to the fresh green scent of an early spring. She spotted the red flash of a fox through the patches of trillium as she watched her father move the tractor about the apple orchard. The sweet smell of the air meant one thing and one thing only to Michiko: baseball season was not far away.

"Did you want to eat anything special for your birthday this year?" her mother asked at breakfast. "We could put in an order with Mr. Nagasaki."

Michiko looked at the ceiling, rolled her eyes, and sighed. Her mother wouldn't even think about making peanut butter and jam sandwiches for lunch, so what was the point? There were so many other things that were always out of the question. Michiko couldn't listen to the girls at school for a minute without hearing about something else her mother wouldn't let her have.

Mary's mother had even bought her grown-up underwear, and she wouldn't be twelve until July.

"I'll let you know," was all Michiko said.

Her father sat down with the newspaper folded in half to show them the advertisement Mr. Downey had placed in the newspaper. He was proud his employer had accepted his suggestion for the last line.

For Sale
Registered Stock Gladiola Bulbs
All Colours — Very Large Blooms
Be Quick Before **We** Plant Them

"If you sell all the bulbs," Michiko said, "you won't have any left to do any work."

Sam smiled and waggled his teacup from side to side. Michiko rose to get the teapot.

"I hope the boss finds someone to give the apple trees their ..." he paused to search for the word he needed in English, "medicine."

Michiko giggled as she handed him his cup. "What kind of medicine?"

Her mother spoke a few words of Japanese to her husband and then turned to Michiko and smiled. "Fruit trees have to be sprayed for bugs," she said as Sam shrugged.

"Is it hard to do?" Michiko asked. "Maybe I could do it."

Both her parents raised their eyebrows.

"I was hoping I could earn some money," Michiko explained.

"Mr. Downey might let you sell strawberries during the summer," Eiko said as she struggled to get Hannah out of her high chair. An envelope fell from the pocket of her apron, and Michiko picked it up. She recognized Mrs. Morrison's spider-like scrawl.

"Just give that to me," her mother said sharply as she passed the baby into Michiko's arms.

"Will he pay me?" Michiko asked, handing her mother the letter.

Her mother took the letter and shoved it into her pocket. "You have to pick them first."

Michiko bounced her little sister up and down as she thought about the envelope. *Why hasn't Mother said anything about hearing from our ghost town friend?* She lowered her sister into the playpen her father had made. Hannah liked to peek through the fancy curved spindles.

Later, as Michiko chased Hiro about the yard, something white stood out on the grass. Michiko bent to pick up the letter her mother had been trying so hard to keep secret. It must have fallen from her pocket. She looked about the yard and headed for the shed. Her eyes raced across the page.

Dear Eiko,

Ralph is enjoying being back on the farm. Sadie stayed with us for a short time after Kaz left, very unhappy about his departure. She told Ralph she didn't care about her husband's participation in the war. I tried to explain that the war causes us all to make sacrifices. Just look what I went through when Ralph was in the navy and lost at sea. You can imagine my look of surprise when she said that Kaz had left her, so she was going to leave too.

I tried to tell her he would eventually come back, but all she would say was, "He will have to find me." I asked her what would happen if he didn't, and she said, "Then we won't be married." She returned to town, and I assumed it was all just talk.

Yesterday a letter from Kaz arrived at our place, and since I was going into town I went to her room at the hotel, but it was empty. Mr. Hayashi told me she went straight to the RCMP with her papers without telling him anything. The rules of the camp are changing daily, so he had no information.

I am so sorry to tell you all this. You may know more than I. If so, please write back to put my mind at ease. These worries travel around my head like a donkey on a stick.

I've enclosed Kaz's letter so that you can forward it on to her. Give everyone my regards. You are all sorely missed.

Edna

P.S. There's a card in the mail for Michiko.

Michiko felt as if a glass of cold water had been thrown in her face. Aunt Sadie had left the ghost town without even telling Mrs. Morrison? Where had she gone? She slipped the folded paper back into its envelope, put it in her pocket, and leaned against the shed wall.

"I was looking for you," Mr. Downey said, startling her.

"My mother said you might let me sell strawberries," Michiko said. "I'd like that."

"Good," he said, "but I had something else in mind. I heard you had a birthday coming."

Michiko nodded.

"There's something in here you might like to use." Mr. Downey reached for a key that lay on top of the doorframe of the shed and turned it in the padlock. They stepped into the dim interior.

Michiko looked around the small building that smelled of dust and rust. What could it be? It took a few minutes for her eyes to adjust from the bright sunlight. At first, all she could see was a couple of wooden crates. Then an object under a canvas tarpaulin came into view.

Mr. Downey tugged at the drape of canvas. "This bicycle has been gathering cobwebs since the Palumbo boy left," he said. "No point in letting it go to waste. Clean it up, and it will be as good as new."

Michiko put her hands to her face in disbelief.

"Can you ride?"

"I'll learn," she replied.

"That's what I thought," he said with a smile. He pulled a wicker basket from the shelf, fixed it to the handlebars, and wheeled it out into the yard. "I have another job for you as well."

"Anything," Michiko said, her eyes widening as she looked at the bike against the tree.

"You are now in charge of picking up all the mail. You will deliver mine to my desk."

"For sure," Michiko said, looking at the silver spokes and large rubber wheels, held together by a chain. "Thanks," she called out to Mr. Downey as he walked away.

It can't be all that hard, Michiko thought as she cleaned the seat off with a rag. Then she took the handlebars and dragged the heavy bike out onto the gravel driveway.

She climbed on to the wide saddle, put her foot on one pedal, and hopped forward, not sure when to lift the other foot off the ground. When she did, the front tire hit a hole and she fell.

Fall down seven times, get up eight, Michiko said to herself. She stood up, wheeled the bike over to the wooden fence, and used the bottom rail to help herself get back on.

With a push of her foot she sailed off down the lane. It felt wonderful to be moving along so easily, but the bike gained speed as it went toward the road. Michiko decided not to pedal forward anymore and lifted her legs, but the bicycle kept on moving. "How do you stop this thing?" she yelled out. In desperation she put her feet back down and pushed backward. The bicycle shrieked and Michiko lurched forward. Both landed in the ditch by the side of the road.

"Need some help?" Eddie asked as he pulled the bike upright.

Michiko brushed the dirt from the palms of her hands. *Why is he always around when I'm in trouble?*

Michiko got up from the ditch and pulled her bike back onto the road.

"Get on," Eddie said as he leaned his bike against the fence. "I'll help you balance."

Michiko had no choice but to listen to his instructions.

He ran a short way alongside her, holding on to the thick wire rack that spanned the back fender. The bike jolted along the pebbly drive. She panicked, jammed on the brakes, and landed on the grass.

"Don't be so hard on the brakes," Eddie said, pulling the frame off of her for a second time. "Before long you'll be cooking with gas! Just keep practising."

He guided her back up to the road. There, Michiko watched him swing his leg over the bar of his own bike and soar toward Mr. Downey's farmhouse with ease.

The next day, she didn't have to be reminded to pick up the mail. She wobbled down the lane on the bike, stuffed the contents of the mailbox into the basket, and wobbled back. Most of it was for Mr. Downey. There was one letter for the Palumbos, and to her surprise two envelopes for her. Michiko recognized the handwriting on both. One was a birthday card from Mrs. Morrison and the other was in writing she had seen often enough across the top of her test papers at school to know exactly whom it was from. She ripped open the envelope.

No. 17 Platoon, B Company
No. 20 Canadian Infantry Training Camp,
Brantford, Ontario
March 15, 1945

Dear Michiko,

How kind of you to write to me. I was getting the feeling everyone had forgotten me. I know your aunt was not happy with my decision, especially the idea of serving a country that has treated us so badly, but everyone has to do their part to bring an end to this war.

There are fifty-three of us, all from B.C., all in one platoon. We are being drilled and taught how to salute, when to say "Sir," and how to make a bed "army style."

I've been fingerprinted, had my picture taken, and been given an ID card. I've also been given a new haircut. You wouldn't believe it.

Our day starts at 6:00 a.m. Our beds have to be made and we are to be dressed and ready to go by 7. We start every week with a route march, leaving the camp at 7:30 and getting back at noon. We march the whole time with only two fifteen-minute breaks. Not too many of us have sore feet, which surprised the officers. I guess it's because we have all been without any kind of transportation for so long, we are really used to walking.

Today is my First Aid Test final, which will end that course and give me a bit more free time. Next time, I won't have to race through my letter like a steam engine.

On Tuesdays we visit the rifle range. We also have to know how to keep a rifle clean. I was very surprised to find out how difficult they are to fire. Yesterday afternoon we got to play some baseball. I wondered if the rifle practice would affect my pitching, but it didn't. How's your pitching arm these days?

I guess as your old teacher, I should ask you about school, but I won't. Do you like Ontario? Have you made lots of new friends? I bet Hannah is growing fast, and

Hiro has found plenty of trees to climb. Please give my best to the rest of your family and have a Happy Birthday.
Kaz

She leaned back and held the letter to her chest. Michiko could hear her uncle's warm, kind voice behind the words and see the crinkles that appeared in the corners of his chocolate brown eyes when he smiled. *But what will happen to that smile and the shine in his eyes when he finds out Sadie has disappeared?* Michiko remembered her teacher saying soldiers counted on good news from home to lift their spirits. *What should I do?*

Michiko wiped her finger across the top of her birthday cake. "Here, Hannah," she said, putting some of the fluffy icing into the baby's mouth.

Hannah licked her lips and smiled. Then she opened her mouth and her arms wide.

"See what you have done," her mother said. "Now Hannah will always want it."

"Always want what?" Sam scooped up the little girl with hair that stuck out like the feathers of a baby bird. "What does my little flower want?"

"Cake," Hiro said with his hands on his hips.

Eiko opened the drawer and handed Michiko a long knife. "You can serve," she said.

As Michiko slid their pieces onto the plates, the smile pasted on her face hid her real feelings about her birthday.

There was no party, as the other girls at school had. Her mother had made her a new skirt, and there was a pair of white knee socks to go with it, but no running shoes.

"Cake!" Hiro demanded. He picked up his fork and banged it on the table.

"Cake, please," Sam said with a smile as he settled his tiny daughter back into her chair. "Happy twelfth birthday, Michiko. Now you can get married."

"Don't be silly," her mother said with a smile. "She has plenty of time for boys."

Her father beckoned her into the living room, where a bedsheet covered a large, boxy shape. Her father removed it with a flourish to present a handmade chest of buffed birch, lined with cedar. Michiko gasped. The *tansu* was a traditional gift for girls that turned twelve. All the Japanese girls in camp talked about filling these hope chests with embroidered pillowcases, dresser scarves, and table cloths. Now Michiko had one too, but the catcher's glove and a pair of running shoes she hoped to put inside it had nothing to do with marriage.

Chapter 15

BATTER UP

Michiko usually ate with Billy, but he wasn't in the lunch room. She spotted his little sister sitting on her own. "Annie," she called, "come and eat with me."

The dandelion-haired little girl piled her lunch into her arms and hurried over.

"Where's Billy?" Michiko asked.

Annie spoke through a mouthful of sandwich. "He's mad at me."

"Why?"

"I can't throw the ball the way he wants," she said. "He yells at me so much, I told him I'm not playing anymore."

Michiko's eyes lit up. "Tell him to come over to my place. I can throw him the ball."

Annie stopped chewing. "Can I come too?"

"Sure," Michiko said. "You can play with Hiro and my baby sister."

Mary plunked a brown paper bag down on the table beside her. Michiko looked up and gave her a wide grin. Her plan of helping Mary at lunchtime was working. "I'd love to see your baby sister," Mary said. "I bet she is really cute."

"Not when you have to change her diaper," Michiko said. "You can come any time you want," she told Mary, but she didn't say it with confidence. She knew Mary lived in a huge, fancy house at the edge of the village. Carolyn was on the same street, quick to point out they faced Lake Ontario, far away from where the lower class lived.

After school, Billy crossed the road carrying his baseball bat, glove, and ball. He used a practice swing to demonstrate his perfect slice.

Michiko tossed the ball in his direction.

Billy let it pass. "Is that the best you can throw?" he jeered as Hiro and Annie ran for it.

Michiko gave him a hard stare.

"Ball one," someone called out. Michiko looked up to see Eddie leaning his bike against the tree. *So that's who's going to help out around the farm,* she thought.

Billy straightened his shoulders at the sight of Eddie and looked to the road. "H-e-a-d-s up!" he yelled to the two tiny outfielders. "This one is bouncing right off the barn."

Something her grandfather used to say popped into Michiko's head as she positioned herself for the next pitch. "Don't value a badger skin before catching the badger," she yelled back. Only she was thinking of the leather skin of the ball.

Michiko threw another ball, and Billy let it go by.

"I could have hit that one if I wanted," he said, "but I'm looking for something meaner."

Eddie took a seat in front of Hiro's jars of bugs that lined the porch. His white T-shirt seemed to glow against his smooth, tanned skin. "Ball two," he yelled out with a grin. "When are you going to stop talking and start swinging?"

Michiko's next ball landed low. Billy swung and blasted a hit down the lane.

"Foul ball," Eddie yelled.

Annie ran to retrieve it.

"I think you are a worse pitcher than my little sister," Billy complained as he leaned on the bat, waiting for Annie to roll them the ball.

Michiko planted her feet in the grass, wound up, and fired the ball at him.

Billy swung and missed.

"Strike two," Eddie called out. He stood, went to his bike, and pulled a leather glove from the handlebar. "I'll catch the next one."

Billy narrowed his eyes and pushed out his lower lip. He put the bat to his shoulder and glared at Michiko. "Put some fire on it," he shouted.

Michiko decided to try one of her Uncle Kaz's specialities. She gripped the ball with her middle fingers, pulled it to her chin, and wound up. Just before she let the ball go, she put the brakes on it. Billy's eyes grew wide at the sight of such an easy hit. He swung so hard, he spun around and fell to the ground.

"You're out," Eddie said as Annie and Hiro fell on the grass, laughing. He turned to Michiko. "Where did you learn to throw like that?"

Michiko thought about her grandfather teaching her to pitch. With a stick, he'd drawn a line from the plate to where she was standing. Then he showed her how to take a step with her front foot, push off with her back, and let the ball fly. It whizzed across the plate, his open fingers pointed at the target. "You do this one thousand times," he said, "step, turn, snap, one thousand times."

One thousand times! Michiko recalled her astonishment. But she did it. Not all in one day, but a couple of hours after school, against the wall of the drugstore, and before she knew it, she could pitch better than the rest of her class, even the boys.

"My grandfather loved baseball," she replied, returning from her thoughts. She didn't bother to mention that her Uncle Kaz had been a professional ball player until the war.

Eddie squinted and studied her face. He picked up the bat and sauntered up to the patch of dirt they used for home plate. "Let's see what you're made of." He tossed Billy his glove. "Isn't that right? Mitch?"

Michiko blinked. *He recognizes me.* She swallowed hard and planted her feet in the grass. Just as she was about to deliver her first pitch, her father and Mr. Downey walked across the front lawn. Sam tapped his boss on the shoulder and pointed. They stood with their arms crossed.

She threw. Eddie let her first pitch pass.

"Ball one," Billy called out.

Michiko threw him a fastball. Eddie swung and missed.

"Strike one," Billy yelled out in glee.

Michiko moved the ball around in her hand. Her father lowered his arms and moved in closer. She took a deep breath, wound up, and let the ball go. Eddie swung and missed.

Her father grinned and elbowed Mr. Downey.

"Strike two," Billy yelled out. "You're in trouble now."

Annie danced about the field, and Hiro copied her.

Michiko remembered what Uncle Kaz had told her about his pitching when he played for the Asahi team: *Always mix it up.*

She threw the ball straight at him, and he tapped it foul.

Eddie's face went red.

Michiko rested her pitching arm against her leg and closed her eyes. If she were to strike him out, he might get angry and say something about giving her a ride home right in front of her father. She opened her eyes when Annie came up with the ball. She grabbed it, holding her fingers in the "okay" position, focussed on Billy's glove, and threw.

Eddie swung and missed.

Billy stood up, looking at the ball in his mitt, with his mouth wide open. Her father gave her a thumbs-up and nudged Mr. Downey again.

Eddie tossed the bat to the ground. He took off his hat. Droplets of sweat sat along his hairline. He wiped his hand across his brow. "Thirsty work, all this striking out."

"Oh," Michiko said. All her mother's advice about how to treat visitors came to her in a rush. "I'll get you a drink of water." She ran into the house and paused at the sink to catch her breath. When she pushed open the screen door, Eddie sat on the porch holding one of Hiro's bug jars.

Michiko handed him the glass with a shaky hand. As she looked into his sky-blue eyes, their fingers touched, making hers tingle.

Eddie grinned as he took it. "I did the same thing when I was a kid," he said. "I had hundreds of bugs in my bedroom."

"Once he came home with the skull of a mouse," Michiko said, relieved Eddie wasn't angry she'd struck him out. "Hiro has to let all the bugs go at night."

"Good thing," Eddie said. "When my snake escaped, my mother went wild." He drained the glass. "Looks like I've got to get to work," he said. Then he walked off toward the orchard.

Michiko tucked her ponytail under her baseball cap and followed Billy out of the parking lot. She was thrilled to be invited to watch him try out for the town team. His dream, like all the other boys trying out, was to play on a winning team. Each year the Bronte Horticultural Society awarded embroidered hats. If Billy's team won, the team caps would have the initials BB on them, for Bronte Braves.

"Hello, Mr. Ward," Billy called out as he waved to one of the teachers when they reached the back of the schoolyard. The grey-haired man, wearing a Yankees cap that had seen a lot of seasons, had a stomach that hung over his belt like a bag of rice. As he hitched up his sagging pants, he eyed Michiko's ball cap.

Billy whispered to Michiko as they walked toward him. "He's a real baseball nut. He had the radio on the whole time we were in gym class just to listen to the World Series."

"I've never seen a cap like that before," the coach said. "What's the team?"

"Asahi," Michiko replied. "Best in the west."

"The west?" Mr. Ward asked. "You mean like Texas?"

Michiko gave him a thin smile. "West of the Rockies," she said.

Billy left her to join the boys on the field. Michiko knew every boy in the district wanted to make the cut. They all had the same hope of working their way up the ranks, playing in front of a scout, and making a professional team. Billy talked nonstop about the St. Louis Cardinals and their World Series results. He'd told her a million times he'd be wearing their white woollen tunic and red striped socks once he finished high school.

Most of her class was there to watch. Mary waved to her from a tartan rug on the grassy mound under a tree at the back of the field. Carolyn sat beside her.

Michiko walked to the blanket and sat down. Her bottom hit something hard. She pulled out Eddie's baseball glove and put it on her lap. Her fingers crept inside, and she opened and closed the leather pouch.

"What do you think you're doing?" Carolyn screeched. "You have no business touching anything that's not yours." She reached across to yank the glove away.

"Feels good, doesn't it?" Eddie asked as he appeared at their side. "My dad sent to the States for it."

"Hi, Eddie," Carolyn said in a high voice as she adjusted the straps of her shoes instead.

Michiko handed Eddie his glove, and he headed toward the field. He turned back and called out, "You can see better from up here."

Michiko stood up to go, but Mary caught her hand and said, "You might get hurt."

"Let her," Carolyn said. "It'll serve her right."

Michiko jogged over to the fence. Her eyes met Eddie's, and he gave her a wink. For some strange reason, her stomach did a flip.

Chapter 16

TRYOUTS

Billy warmed up with a couple of pitches as they watched from the sidelines.

"They've put him on the mound to see what he's made of," Eddie said. "Hopefully all your coaching has paid off."

"He knows where the plate is," Michiko said.

Mr. Ward pawed through a couple of pages on a clipboard and then looked up. "Donald Maitland up to bat," he called out.

Donald stepped up to the plate. Billy struck him out. Donald slung his bat in despair and went back to the bench.

"Robert Wells," Mr. Ward called out.

"Bobby can really hit," Eddie told her. "He was on the team last year."

Billy threw two strikes. On the third pitch, Bobby hit a sharp bounce to Billy's right. He caught it, spun left, and threw it to first.

"Out," yelled the coach.

Bobby looked at Billy as if he had just seen him for the first time and left for the bench.

Jimmy Johnston was next at bat. He hit it high but short. Billy raised his hands for the catch, took a step backward, and stumbled. Michiko's fingers flew to her face as Billy's arms moved at his sides like a windmill. He went down, but the ball landed in his glove.

"Way to go," Eddie called out.

Coach Ward blew his whistle, sent Billy to the bench, and consulted his clipboard. "That's it?" He looked around and then walked over to Michiko and Eddie. "You trying out?"

"Not for Junior League," Eddie answered with a grin.

"Not you, numbskull," the coach said, "your buddy, the one that played ball out west." He leaned in front of Eddie and hollered at Michiko. "Hey kid, what's your name?"

Her eyes widened.

"It's Mitch," Eddie told the coach. He turned to Michiko with a huge grin.

"You want to play baseball?" the coach asked. "I'm trying to make an even dozen."

Michiko turned and looked at Eddie with surprise.

"You want to play?" he asked her.

She nodded.

Eddie pushed her shoulder. "Then get on that mound."

"Okay, Mitch," the coach bawled out as he walked away. "You're at bat. Bobby, you can pitch. Mark, let's see you as catcher. You five in the field. Let's play some ball."

Michiko pulled down her uncle's baseball cap, making sure it was on good and tight. It was a bit large for her, but she was thankful for that, with all the hair stuffed inside. As she walked past the coach, he gave her a hard slap on the back, and she fell forward toward the bench. Billy jumped up in surprise when he saw her stumble toward him.

Michiko threw him a warning glance, and he sat back down with a thud.

Bobby put the ball into his mitt, raised it to his chin, and gave her a hard look.

She let his first ball go by. *Too low,* she thought and swung her bat to show him where she wanted the ball.

The next ball barely missed her ear as it whizzed past her head, but she didn't swing. *What is he thinking?* she wondered as the catcher tossed the ball back. *If he makes me walk, it only looks bad for him.* Out of the corner of her eye she glanced at Eddie. Coach Ward, standing beside him, was writing on his clipboard.

On the next pitch, Michiko sent the ball soaring out into the field. She dashed to first base. There she took a deep breath and turned to see the play. *So far, so good.* Someone fumbled it in the field. She ran again. At second, Eddie gave her a thumbs-up.

The next batter swung wildly at the first two balls. He hit it far enough for her to make it to third base.

The catcher raised his facemask and laughed when the next batter was out at first, but he missed the ball on its return. As he watched it roll away, Michiko stole home. The boys on the bench all stood up in surprise.

Mr. Ward wrote on his clipboard again.

The second time Michiko got up to bat, she swung so hard, she had to catch herself from falling over. She fouled the next ball and her heart sank. She swung at the third in panic.

"'Yer out," the umpire called out.

She heard the catcher snicker under his mask.

Her grandfather's voice came into her head as she walked to the field. *Accomplishments remain with oneself.* She knew they were all thinking that she was no good.

Michiko spent the next couple of hours in centre field under the hot summer sun. She tipped her head back and forth but didn't dare take off her hat to shake her hair free. Her feet, encased in her leather farm boots, felt like they were baking in an oven.

The bat cracked. Michiko looked up and walked backward, keeping her eye on the tiny white blur as it got closer and closer. She was directly under it when the white ball seemed to disappear in the sun's brightness. She squinted, opened her glove, and heard the ball drop. When she looked down, it was in her mitt.

The kids on the bench roared in approval.

Her hopes were high until the coach moved her off the field back on to the bench.

Something cold hit her shoulder and she looked around. Eddie stood beside her with a large grin. "Catch this," he said. "You need a cool down." He threw another piece of ice at her. Michiko caught it and rubbed it across the back of her neck.

Donald went up to bat again and hit the ball high. As Michiko shaded her eyes against the sun, she saw a blur flying toward her face, but before she could get out of the way, she felt the ball's hard crushing blow as she slid to the ground.

The first thing she saw when she tried to open her eye was Eddie's furrowed brow. Coach Ward stood behind him. "You okay?"

Michiko sat up, but the world swam. She put her hand to her face, clenching her teeth together. Her forehead and right cheek pounded, but she didn't dare cry.

"You're lucky you didn't get knocked out," Eddie said, taking her by the elbow to help her stand. He let her catch her breath and then led her to the parking lot.

"What happened?" Mary asked, racing to their side when she saw them.

Carolyn followed. "I told you she would get hurt."

Eddie opened the door of his father's big black sedan. "I'll take you home."

Michiko's headache and the bright summer sun reduced her world to such a small space, she could hardly see to get in the car.

"We're supposed to be going for ice cream," Carolyn whined. "Why can't she just wait for Billy's father to come back?"

Mary shot her a look of disgust. "First we are going to take her home," she said, "and then my father's going to go to her house and take a look. You can stay here."

Eddie leaned in, removed Michiko's hand from her red, swollen eye and gave her a handkerchief of cold ice. He was so close, she could smell his spearmint gum. "My dad's a doctor," he whispered. "Everything will be fine."

Not trusting herself to speak, Michiko could only nod, and even that brought pain. She slumped back against the seat, holding the handkerchief against her eye.

Dr. Adams, a tall, plain-faced man with dark hair and the scent of aftershave, folded his stethoscope into his deep, dark, square-bottomed bag and said, "I've given her a full check-up. She's in perfect health. No damage to the eye, but she will have a nasty bruise. A few days off school will allow for the swelling to go down."

Sam saw him to the door as Eiko administered another cold compress.

Just as Michiko drifted off to sleep, she felt a rough hand at her chin. "I probably didn't even make the team," she mumbled to her father.

"You'll get on the team," Sam responded, patting her head. "You got my arm. But you sure gonna have a shiner," he added. "Good thing Sadie isn't here. She'd laugh a lot at you."

Michiko felt the sting of her tears. If only she knew where Sadie was.

"What happened to you?" the librarian asked as she stared at Michiko's rainbow-coloured face when they returned their books on Saturday.

"I got hit with a ball," Michiko said, pulling the bill of her baseball cap lower.

Annie pressed her small hands to the sides of her face and frowned. "Does it hurt a lot?"

"Not too bad," Michiko replied.

"Baseball is stupid," Annie said, crossing her arms and turning to the window.

"Better get used to it," Billy said, throwing his cap on to the table. "We're going to play every single day of spring break."

Michiko waited a long time for Billy to turn up for their usual game of catch. The sharp odour of cow manure filled her nostrils as she biked up his laneway to see what was keeping him. She found him on the steps of the long front porch, which sagged like an old couch, with his head in his hands. His dirt-streaked cheeks made her think he'd been crying. She waited a few moments before she spoke. "Aren't we going to practise?"

"Nope," he said, his head still in his hands. "Annie threw my baseball in the lake. She had to go to her room until my mom decides how to punish her." He stood up and kicked the porch. "But that doesn't bring my ball back."

Michiko sat in silence, studying the ground. She noticed a bottle cap and nudged it with her toe to see what it said. She reached down, picked it up, and put it in her pocket.

"What are you going to use that for?" Billy asked, raising his head.

"Hiro collects bottle caps," she said. "I don't think he has an Orange Crush."

Billy stood up. "Come on," he said as they walked behind the cow barn to a large, red metal box. "My dad fixed up this old cooler because he was tired of walking to the house for a cold drink." He pulled the handle on the front panel and removed a tin trough. "Help yourself," he said. "We've got thousands."

"Thousands?" Michiko repeated in awe.

Billy took the trough to the wooden box beside the machine. "See?" he said as he dumped the bottle caps on top of the already rusting pile. "It's not always soda pop," he explained. "My dad puts in whatever he feels like drinking."

Michiko picked out a bottle cap and gave it a toss in the air. Her eyes widened with an idea. She turned and scuffed out four lines in the dirt yard with the heel of her boot. "Single, double, triple, and home run," she told Billy. "Go get your bat."

Billy grinned. "First we need a strike zone," he said, picking up a stick and dipping it in the scummy water around the cow trough. He marked a muddy square on the wall of the barn.

It took them a few moments of practice to get the caps skimming through the air using a sidearm toss, until their game of bottle-cap baseball began, and Billy knew exactly who was going to have to pick them all up.

Michiko rode through the dandelion-dotted orchard along the tiny path that led directly to shore. The bicycle squeaked as she pedalled through the fishy smell of the water's edge. The surface of Lake Ontario was a blanket of fine wrinkles.

She jumped off to walk the bicycle, along the narrow stretch of beach where the sand was too soft to manage, until she reached the parking lot beside the harbour. There she remounted and headed for the school.

Billy rode up the sweep of gravel that led to the school, leaning forward like a dog on a hunt for a rabbit.

"Where did you get the bike?" Michiko asked. His was much newer than hers.

"My dad picked it up at an auction. It's a reward for that A on my report card."

Billy ran his finger down the team list posted on the glass of the school's front door. "I made the team," he yelled and did a victory dance in front of the window.

Michiko approached the list with caution. Striking out at a tryout was nothing to be proud of, but Eddie had told her not to give it another thought. She ran her finger down the list. There it was, her third name since leaving Vancouver. "So did I," she said with a grin. "Or at least Mitch did," and she did a couple of cartwheels across the grass, her long, dark pigtails smacking her in the face.

They walked across the grass to the trees on the hill and lay on the grass with their legs crossed. "I can't wait to see Carolyn's face when she finds out you're a ball player."

"You can't tell her," Michiko said, sitting up. "She'll try to stop me from playing."

Billy grimaced. "You're right," he said. "She is such a troublemaker."

"Don't say anything to anyone," Michiko cautioned, "not even Annie."

"But Annie will know if you talk about going to the games."

"Just tell her I'm your coach." Michiko rubbed the spot above her eye where the ball had hit her. "Tell her I only want to watch — because I got hit."

Billy nodded. Then he picked up his bike.

Michiko paused to stuff her pigtails underneath her cap.

"You better get rid of all that hair," Billy said when she picked up her handlebars.

Michiko put a hand to the back of her head. "I'll have to think about that," she said as she pushed off. In her house, cutting one's hair above the ear was considered shocking and rebellious. She'd just have to tie it up really tight.

"I'll race you to the Esso station," Billy said.

Chapter 17

SADIE

The excitement of making the team turned Michiko's legs into pumping pistons. She pedalled hard to beat Billy to the gas station, and she did. After a breather, she rode home, picked up the mail, and headed for Mr. Downey's back door. "I'm back," she called out to her mother, but got no answer. Hannah wasn't in her playpen, and there was no sign of Hiro either. She placed Mr. Downey's mail on the kitchen table beside a new Eaton's catalogue. *That's funny,* she thought. *He must have taken it from the mailbox himself.*

Michiko peeked down the hallway but saw no one. Mrs. Downey's toaster sat on the counter. She couldn't resist pushing down the lever and peeking inside the silver box to see the wiggly wire elements turn ruby red. Then she closed the side door and walked to the clothesline beside the vegetable garden. But there was no sign of her mother there, either.

Mrs. Palumbo stood in her shapeless print housedress with her hands on her hips, waiting for the watering can to fill. She looked up and scowled in Michiko's direction, but Michiko could no longer contain herself. She had to tell someone her news. She ran up to Mrs. Palumbo, grabbed her hands, and swung them back and forth.

"Mrs. Palumbo," she said, "I made the team. Isn't that great? I made the team."

The woman furrowed her brow, making the knot of her back hairnet rise above the crevice on her forehead.

Michiko dropped the woman's hands and took the stance of holding a bat in front of the puzzled old lady. "Baseball, Mrs. Palumbo." She swung her bat and put her hand to her forehead as she watched her imaginary ball soar into the stands. "I made the baseball team."

Mrs. Palumbo's watery, pale blue eyes lit up in comprehension. "*Si*," she said, "base-a-ball." Then she took a stance herself and pretended to whack a ball with a bat. She pointed her finger and traced her imaginary ball across the sky. "Home-a-run."

"That's right," Michiko said as she tapped her chest. "I'm going to hit a lot of home runs." Michiko could picture a small shelf of trophies like her Uncle Kaz's.

To her surprise, Mrs. Palumbo's whole face transformed. She smiled so wide, the straight lines at the corners of her mouth disappeared. She raised her gnarled hands and patted her chest. "*Mi filio*," she said, "Antonio, base-a-ball." Then, as if she suddenly remembered something sad, her smile dropped and she turned to haul the can into the garden.

Michiko went back to retrieve her bike. She thought about the Eaton's catalogue. Maybe she could make enough money picking strawberries to buy a pair of running shoes. She pushed her bike toward the shed just as her mother's angry voice rose from the open front window.

"Not talking about it doesn't make it go away. Isn't that what you told me yourself?"

Michiko froze.

"I am not talking about it anymore," a voice Michiko could barely hear replied. "Besides, it wasn't as if I was really married."

"What exactly is that supposed to mean?" Eiko screeched so loud that Michiko gripped her handlebars.

"You know exactly what I mean," the soft voice said. "There was no formal consent, no go-between conference, gifts, or dowry accepted."

"So *now* you decide to be Japanese. All your life you fight your heritage, and now you've decided to embrace it completely. What have you become, a *ronin?* Wandering the countryside without your *shogun* master? You were married by a minister in a church. Are you telling me that doesn't count!"

It was Aunt Sadie! But it didn't sound as if her mother was too happy about it. Michiko laid her bike on the grass and tiptoed to the kitchen door. Sadie's purse, a green snakeskin box that had a gold triangle-shaped clasp, sat on the table.

"Mom," Michiko called out. "Guess what! I made the team!" She let the screen door slam as she went inside, something she wasn't supposed to do. "Hey, Hiro," she called out. "Are you going to watch me play?"

When her mother entered the kitchen, Michiko pretended not to notice her flushed face.

"Don't be so noisy," she said. "Hiro and Hannah are with your father." Her mother filled the kettle and placed it on the stove. "Go and find them. Tell your father we'll have tea."

"Is that Michiko?" the voice in the living room said.

Michiko looked at her mother and raised her eyebrows.

Eiko rolled her eyes to the ceiling. "Yes," she said. "It is your Aunt Sadie, unexpected, unannounced, and unprepared."

Sadie gave Michiko a hug and then held her at arms' length as if she needed to see what was different. But instead of warmth, Michiko got a feeling of boniness. Aunt Sadie had always been fashionably slim, but she'd never felt like a skeleton before. This was definitely not the lady who wouldn't dream of going anywhere without lipstick. She had small lines at the corners of her mouth and eyes. Not only was her lipstick missing, it was as if she had given up her flowery scent altogether.

Eiko forced her face into a smile. "A letter came from Kaz," she said. "Edna sent it."

Sadie said nothing. She paid a great deal of attention to her hands, adjusting her gold wedding band. Then she turned to look out the window and gave a tinny laugh, the kind that sounded like there were tears behind it. "That's nice," she said.

Eiko removed the letter from the pocket of her apron and slid it across the table.

Sadie turned it face down.

That evening, Michiko watched her aunt sweep Hiro off his feet to say goodnight. He squirmed in her arms until she lowered him to the floor. Then she leaned over the crib to kiss Hannah. Sadie took a deep breath. "How I miss that baby smell," she said with a deep sigh.

After her homework, Michiko tiptoed into the kitchen with their spare blanket and pillow. Sadie was to sleep on the couch in their living room. She had offered to give up her bed, but her mother shook her head. Michiko watched her aunt pull off her earrings and place them on her handkerchief beside Kaz's letter.

"Aren't you going to read it?" Michiko asked.

"I don't have to," Sadie said. "I know what it says." She rose from her chair and went to the stove. She held the envelope to the burner, and then she carried it to the sink to watch the flames consume it.

Michiko watched in horrified silence.

Sadie turned to her and gave her a tired smile. "Good night," she whispered.

The next morning, the distant murmur of the radio punctuated by her father's cheers told her he was celebrating the highlights of yesterday's ball game. Her aunt's voice came from her mother's bedroom across the hall as she sang to Hannah. The banging coming from the other side of her wall meant Hiro was playing with his cat.

When Michiko came into the kitchen, Sadie was sitting at the kitchen table in her mother's wine-coloured dressing robe with Hannah on her lap. Michiko studied her aunt's face in the bright daylight. She had dark circles under her eyes and did not bubble over with her usual fun. Her feet were bare.

Michiko remembered the time her aunt had stopped by their house wearing a red satin dress and glittering necklace. Sadie had let Michiko try on her black patent high heels, and Michiko couldn't stop turning them one way and another to admire their shine.

"Did you bring your wedding shoes with you?" Michiko asked. Her aunt had worn the most beautiful pair of white satin pumps on her special day.

"I couldn't," Sadie said, turning to her without a smile. "I only owned part of them."

"What do you mean?"

One hand went to her aunt's face while the other fingered the robe. "Before I got married, four of the teachers discovered we all wore the same size shoe. Each of us put in $1.50 to buy those satin pumps. Whoever got married next wore them."

"Who got them next?"

Sadie shrugged. "Someone who is more suited to be a wife."

"What is that supposed to mean?" Eiko asked, putting down her cup with a small thud.

Sadie fingered her hair. "I told you I am not talking about it anymore."

Sam withdrew his attention from the radio and came to sit at the table. He rattled his teacup. Eiko reached for the pot and refilled it.

Sadie pushed a bowl of dry cereal toward him.

"Where's my rice?" he asked.

"This *is* rice," Sadie said, "toasted rice cereal."

Sam lifted the spoon to his mouth. "Pah," he said, pushing the bowl aside. "It tastes like crackers. Give me a bowl of rice."

"I am not preparing rice for breakfast anymore," Eiko said, pushing the sugar bowl toward him. "Try it with a bit of sugar."

Sam shoved the bowl of sugar away. "A meal without rice is not a meal."

Sadie pushed it back. "Do you like your children being laughed at by others?"

Sam frowned. "No."

"They are Canadian," she said quietly. "Canadian children eat cereal for breakfast. Pour some milk over it and see what happens."

Sam poured milk over the crispy nubs in his bowl and perked up. He put his ear to the bowl. "Listen," he said. "The cereal is talking."

"What?" Hiro said, his slice of toast stopping halfway to his mouth.

"It is saying, 'Don't eat me, don't eat me.'"

Michiko leaned her head close to her bowl of cereal. It was true. Her cereal was also making a faint crackling sound. "It's asking me how long you are going to stay, Aunt Sadie."

Hiro looked into his empty cereal bowl, puzzled. "Why did it talk?"

"So you won't be lonely at breakfast," Sadie said.

"Mine just said, 'I'm going back on Saturday.' That is if Sam can give me a lift?"

"He's going to drive you to B.C.?" Michiko's mouth fell open.

"To Toronto, silly," her aunt replied. "That's where I live."

"You do?" Michiko had no idea her aunt had been so close all this time.

"I got a part-time job in a department store," Sadie said, refilling her own teacup. "In fact, I was just suggesting to your mother that you visit me at the store."

"Really?" Michiko asked, turning to her mother. She couldn't believe her ears. Her aunt had just invited her to go to Toronto. *I'll bet Mary's never been to Toronto*, she thought. But when she saw her mother's tight face, she knew it was not the time to talk about it.

Eiko rose to the sound of a knock at the door.

Mrs. Palumbo stuck her head in the door and beckoned Michiko outside with her long, bony finger. From behind her back, the woman pulled out a pair of beat-up black-and-white shoes.

"*Scarpe*," she said, handing them to Michiko. Then she took a stance and pretended to whack a ball with a bat. She pointed her finger and said, "Home-a-run."

Michiko threw her arms around the woman's aproned waist and hugged her tight. They couldn't be more perfect. They were boy's runners.

Chapter 18

DEAR GERALD

Michiko could hardly take her eyes off her feet as she pedalled toward the schoolyard. Who would have thought she'd be wearing *the shoes of champions*? What did the advertisement in the newspaper say? "*In every game where you have to cover ground fast, athletes play in the shoe that is build for speed.*" She grinned. Her mother was so impressed with their tough, springy soles and heavy canvas tops, she'd bought Michiko a new pair of laces.

The glorious Saturday sun that stretched out across the bright blue sky made Michiko glad to be alive and even gladder to be heading to a baseball practice. A cloud shaped like a cake made her laugh out loud. *Perfect,* she thought, *a cake to celebrate getting on the team.*

At the front of the school, her nose filled with the scent of lush lilacs. The willows in the back waved their new budding greenery as she and Billy dropped their bikes and walked to the crowd of players. She recognized Donald Maitland, Kenny Spencer, and Mark McAndrew from the class at the other end of the hall. Bobby Wells, the next grade up, had made the team for a second year, which didn't surprise her. The others were what Billy called "Other Towners," meaning they lived in the country but went to school in the village.

"Everyone gather around," Coach Ward called out as he waddled over to the worn, initial-carved bench and dropped the battered duffle bag he had dragged across the grass. From it he pulled a bent catcher's mask, some ragged shin pads, and a quilted chest protector that reminded her of her mother's worn oven mitts. Four bats, each a different colour and size, landed on the grass next to a pile of baseball gloves. Everyone grabbed a mitt, leaving the worn, unravelled lefty for her.

"Ready to toss?" the coach hollered.

Billy kicked at the grass. "Lost my ball," he said.

The coach nodded in the direction of the bag. Billy searched the interior to find a ratty one tucked in the far corner. The rest of the team had formed two lines and was tossing balls back and forth. Michiko stood alone, not knowing what to do.

"We throw the ball back and forth until the coach blows the whistle," Billy said. "If neither of us has dropped it, we move back two steps. Otherwise, we stay put until the next whistle."

Michiko nodded. It seemed easy enough.

Coach Ward walked to the bench, pulled a newspaper from the equipment bag, and sat down. Michiko soon realized that he'd blown the whistle before he turned to the next page. She and Billy moved apart with each short, sharp blast. The coach didn't seem to notice that they were farther apart than any of the others when he finally finished reading his paper. He threw it into the duffle bag, pulled out a newer, larger bat, and waved them into the field.

At the plate, Coach Ward tossed the ball into the air and hit it with a loud thwack. The ball soared into the air as the players lifted their arms and opened their gloves.

On his third hit, the ball headed in Michiko's direction. Kenny was close by. Michiko moved away to let him have it, but the ball ended up on the grass.

"Call the darn ball," the coach bellowed. He bent over, picked up another ball from the pile, and belted it into the air. This time it came straight for her. "Mine," she yelled and opened her glove. She squinted her eyes against the sun as it rushed toward her. The ball hit her mitt with a thud and then rolled onto the grass.

Michiko looked at it and scowled. This time the coach blew his whistle twice. "Line up at the mound," he said, tossing the first player a ball.

Coach Ward tied the catcher's apron around himself and pulled on the mask. He crouched behind home plate and punched the mitt to let them know he was ready for pitching practice.

Michiko threw easily at first, making sure she warmed up the way her Uncle Kaz had taught her. As she felt her arm loosen, she threw harder, threw straight through the strike zone, right into his mitt.

"Wow," someone said, making the team gather around to watch.

The coach dropped his hand and pointed two fingers to the ground. Michiko held the ball and looked at Billy.

He cupped his mouth with his hands and yelled, "It means throw a fastball."

Michiko rolled the ball around in her hand before putting it into her glove. Then she blazed it across the plate. When it landed in the coach's glove, everything felt so good.

Mr. Ward blew his whistle and the players dropped to the grass. He made notes on his clipboard while they waited.

Please don't put me in centre field, Michiko pleaded as she raised her eyes to the sky. A tiny bead of perspiration formed on her forehead and started to make its way down her nose. She wiped it away with her sleeve. She desperately wanted to take off her hat and shake her hair free.

She picked a dandelion but threw it down quickly. *Boys don't pick flowers*, she reminded herself.

"That's all for today," the coach announced, walking away dragging the equipment bag.

Michiko looked around. The only one left in the field was Billy. *So what was her position?* She had spent so much time daydreaming, she hadn't heard.

"Maybe your dad will buy you one," Billy said, as he walked toward her.

"One what?"

"A pitcher needs a glove," Billy said.
Michiko did a cartwheel.

A single letter waited inside the metal mailbox at the top of the lane.

Dear Michiko,

Army food isn't too bad. Sausages for dinner, bacon for breakfast, but the eggs are powdered. Classes are from 8:00 to 4:30 and 7:00 to 9:00 at night. Wednesday afternoons are for military training. There's a kind of recess break at 3:30 where we get sent outside no matter what the weather. It's supposed to keep us alert, but some of the guys complain.

At 11:00 it is "lights out," the army's way of getting us used to the darkness of war. All of the J-C's find this funny since we lived by lanterns and candles in the ghost towns. It's easy for us to study by flashlights. Some of the guys use the nightlights in the washrooms.

We have courses in reading, writing, and speaking Japanese. They gave us seven books. All of us start with a school primer. We also study geography and mapping.

I got 100 percent in my elementary language test and they bumped me to the advanced class. Now I work at translating selections from Japanese middle school texts, essays, magazine articles, and even plays. I have to carry a heavy Japanese dictionary with me everywhere I go. We have study periods from 9:00 p.m. to 10:00 p.m., four nights a week, with examinations every Saturday.

I'm also training as a radio announcer and speech writer. Sadie should be the one here for that as she could always come up with cleverer sayings than me.

To put your mind at rest, not all graduates of the Language School are sent into combat, even though I had hoped for some real action. Some of us will remain at school for further training. They keep saying our weapons are language, skill, and intelligence, not machine guns and bayonets. You remember that.

Kaz

Michiko couldn't wait to tell Uncle Kaz she was pitcher on the baseball team. She could just see the smile creep across his face when he read her news. She folded the paper and slid it back inside the envelope. *Should I tell Kaz about Sadie moving to Toronto when I write back?* A black squirrel that had climbed down from the tree near the fence sat statue-still on the grass, as if it was waiting for her answer. She stuffed the letter into the pocket of her overalls, looked at the squirrel, and shrugged. Her father's voice echoed in her head: "*This is adult business, you stick to kid business.*"

"There's twelve on the team," she told them all at the dinner table. "Coach Ward calls us his dirty dozen." She knew her mother would frown when she heard that, and she did, but Michiko just kept on talking. "Only six of us are from the village. The rest of the team comes from farms roundabout. Our practices are behind our school. The first game is next Saturday at three o'clock." Michiko knew she was talking fast, but she had to get all of the information out of the way before she made her big announcement.

"Coach give out positions yet?" her father asked.

Michiko picked up her chopsticks, lowered her eyes, and waited.

"Everyone is important," he said with concern in his eyes. "Doesn't matter what it is."

"I know," she said, but couldn't stand her own suspense. "I'm just the pitcher."

"Just the pitcher?" her father repeated with a huge smile. He stood up and clapped his hands. Hannah looked up from the bits of food on her tray and copied him.

"Come-grat-you-lations," her father said. His eyes shone.

"I just need to get a glove," Michiko announced in what she hoped was a casual voice.

"Those are expensive," her mother said. "We'll have to think about that."

"Can't you borrow one?" Sadie asked.

"Doesn't matter where it comes from," Michiko said, looking at her father. "A pitcher needs a glove, right, Dad?"

Her father gave a solemn nod but made no promises.

After dinner, Michiko spotted Eddie in the yard and went outside to tell him.

"Congratulations," he said as he pulled his bike away from the tree. "Maybe they'll win a few games." He took something from his pocket and tossed it toward her. "Have a look at this. It's a Spalding, and the centre is cork."

Michiko caught the cold, white leather ball that was so perfect and clean. She ran her thumb over the seam. The stitching was bright red. The baseball reminded her to ask. "Is there such a thing as a one-armed pitcher in the league?"

"Yup," Eddie answered. "Pete Gray, number 14 for the St. Louis Browns. I read about him on the sports page."

"How did he lose his arm?" she asked as she handed him back the baseball.

"Truck accident," Eddie said. "He tosses the ball into the air, tucks the glove into his armpit, catches the ball, and fires it off."

"What about hitting?" Michiko's couldn't contain her amazement.

"He plants the knob of the bat against his side and bunts." Then he rode off.

Michiko's father often said Eddie was a good worker. She hoped Mr. Downey would give him more to do so he would hang around, but in the meantime she had the information she wanted. She'd be able to tell all her soldiers about this amazing ball player.

Michiko placed the thin piece of blue airmail paper over a page of her workbook. She liked to use the shadow of the lines underneath to keep her writing straight. She had just finished telling Gerald about Pete Gray when her aunt stuck her head around the corner.

"What are you doing?" she asked.

Michiko's hand slid to her overall pocket to make sure Kaz's envelope was safely tucked out of sight. "I'm writing to a serviceman," she said.

"Really?" her aunt said as she came closer. "Why is that?"

"Servicemen need to get mail, even if it's from a stranger." She paused for a moment and said, "It's really hard for them to be far away from their family and friends."

Her aunt put her hand to her throat and fingered the top button of her blouse. "What kinds of things do you say?"

"I just give them the news from home, what we kids are doing for the war effort … things like that." She pointed to the letter she had just begun. "Gerald asked me about the one-armed baseball player in the American League. He says the news they get is old and all mixed-up, and I'm telling him all about Pete Gray." Michiko looked her aunt in the eye. "You could tell Uncle Kaz about him. I've got extra paper if you want."

Sadie's lashes fluttered.

Michiko looked down, pretending to be interested in her work. "Don't forget to tell him that I'm pitcher for the team."

Sadie left the room.

Michiko opened the little blue box on her desk and slid Kaz's letter underneath the others before going back to her writing.

A lot of the baseball players are in uniform like you. Joe DiMaggio is my dad's favourite player. He had a picture of him on our kitchen wall, but my mother made him take it down. I have an uncle in uniform who loves baseball, too. Thanks for asking the question about Pete Gray. Now I can tell my uncle all about him, too. We have a junior league and a senior league in town. Both of them are called the Bronte Braves. One of the boys that works on our farm plays for the senior league. He just got a Spalding baseball. He said the middle of it is made of cork.

Her mother popped her head into her room. "It's getting late," she said.

I am running out of space. I hope you'll write back. I'll try to find the answers to all your baseball questions. I hope the war isn't too bad for you.

Millie

She signed the letter with a flourish, folded it, slid it into its envelope, and addressed it. On Monday morning she would give it to Mrs. McIntosh for the collection bag.

Chapter 19

THE FIRST GAME

Michiko saw the white paper edge sticking out of her mathematics book when she returned to her desk after recess. *Will it be another nasty drawing?* she wondered as she pulled at the paper corner. The postcard of a little doll holding an announcement card surprised her. She turned it over and read:

Because it's my birthday there's going to be
A party at our house just for me!
Here is the time (2–4 P.M.)
And here is the date (May 5)
Please come and help me to celebrate.
Mary Margaret Adams

For a moment Michiko couldn't breathe. Was it really what she thought it was, or just another trick? She glanced around to see if Carolyn was around.

She wasn't. Michiko slipped the card into her exercise book.

On the bus she leaned back and closed her eyes. *A birthday party at Mary's house.* Mary, checking to see if she had received it, told her she would get to meet her mother since she already knew her father and her brother. She felt her heart beat faster and her face flush at the thought of Eddie being there. Whenever she saw him, a warm, feathery feeling came over her.

Michiko showed the invitation to Aunt Sadie that night.

"How nice," Sadie said. "Do you know this girl well?"

"She sits beside me at school," Michiko explained. "I can't believe she invited me. She's one of ..." she faltered, not quite knowing how to put it, "... of the girls in town."

"I know these girls," Sadie said.

"You do?" *Aunt Sadie has been here only a few days. How can she have gotten to know Mary and her town friends?*

"They live in the expensive houses, wear nice clothes, and spend their summers boating," Sadie explained. "You find these girls in every town."

"There were no girls like that where we last lived," Michiko said.

Sadie reached for her niece's hand and patted it. "You were that girl in our last town, silly. You just didn't know it."

"I was?"

"You didn't notice that all the other girls envied your extra special clothes and malted milks at the drugstore."

"I didn't get to drink them," Michiko said. "You know that." Whenever she thought of milkshakes, she thought of George King making a big production of counting out his change in front of her father. "And there was nothing extra special about my clothes," she added.

"Think about Kiko," her aunt said in a low voice.

The girl with the uncombed hair who wore summer clothes all year long floated up in front of Michiko's face. Their friendship had come to an end over a stolen watch. Kiko had no mother or father, only an uncle who tried to look after her the best he could.

"But all my clothes were homemade," Michiko protested. "Nothing came from a store."

"They didn't know that," Sadie said. "They looked at your life and looked at theirs and decided yours was better. Everyone does it. You are probably thinking right now that Mary's life is so much better than yours."

Michiko looked at her aunt in surprise. Sadie always had the knack of knowing exactly what was on her mind.

"And," her aunt said as she rose from the couch, "I bet you are also wondering what you are going to wear? That was always the first thing on my mind whenever I got an invitation."

"I don't have to wonder about that," Michiko said. "I'll just have to wear what is clean."

"To a party?" Sadie stood, took Michiko's hand, and pulled her up from the couch. "You will not just wear whatever is clean, not while I am here."

Michiko looked up at her aunt's shining eyes. "Really?"

Michiko could hardly sit still in the back of Billy's car. Every part of her body was alive with excitement. Playing baseball was like meeting up with a best friend.

The visiting team was on the field warming up when they arrived. Michiko's father, Mr. Palumbo, and Billy's father walked to the first base line to watch.

Michiko stopped for a moment to ram her hat down on her head when Mr. Ward called out, "Bring it in." Her team formed a circle to get their very first pregame pep talk. She was expecting a lot more than, "You all know what to do," before Coach Ward stuck his hand into the centre and everyone piled theirs on top. "Good luck," she whispered to Billy as they ran out to the field. He winked back.

The batter hit Michiko's first pitch right through the shortstop's legs, and he made it to first before they got the ball there.

She threw to the next batter. Michiko thought he hit foul, but the umpire called it fair, and the other team now had runners on first and second. Her third pitch brought them all home with a hit clear across the playground into the parking lot. The crowd sitting in camp chairs around the baseball diamond stood up and cheered.

Michiko looked around at the other members of her team. They all scowled at the 3–0 score. Then she spotted Eddie standing next to Billy's dad. Eddie nodded and gave his whole body a shake. *He's right,* she thought. *Like Uncle Kaz used to say, shake it off.*

She struck out the next three batters, and before they knew it, the Bronte Braves were at the plate.

Up first, Michiko got a hit and made it to first. She could hear her father cheering from the sidelines. Billy hit a grounder, which got her to third, and him to second, but the visiting team's right fielder caught their next player's pop fly, making it one out with runners on second and third. Donald Maitland, whom everyone knew was a strong hitter, was up next.

The pitcher for the opposite team studied Donald for a moment, pulled back his arm, and sent the ball across the plate. Donald swung hard, and they all heard that wonderful "thunk" of wood hitting a ball. He took off like a bullet, as did Billy and Michiko. Then the umpire called out, "Strrrike one, foul ball."

"No foul," she heard her father yell.

Michiko's cheeks burned as they returned to their plates. *He isn't going to cause trouble by arguing with the umpire, is he?*

The pitcher for the opposing team pulled back his arm and sent the ball across the plate a second time. Donald hit it with a resounding crack, and Michiko made it home.

Kenny Spencer, next at bat, raised his chin and hunched his body, determined to get a home run. He hit the ball, but the player at first base caught it, tagged the plate, and threw it to the pitcher before Kenny reached the plate.

But his throw wasn't strong enough.

Michiko signalled Billy to steal the base as the pitcher sauntered into the field to pick up the ball. The smile on the pitcher's face froze when he saw Billy heading straight past him for third. He grabbed at the ball but fumbled it. The crowd roared as he picked it up a second time and threw it home. Billy dove into the dust and touched the plate before the catcher tagged him on the ankle.

"Safe," the umpire shouted.

The kids on the Braves bench went wild.

One more run and the score would be tied, but their next player didn't make it to third. Three strikeouts in a row brought them out to the field, and it was Michiko's turn to face the batters again.

She threw the ball right across the plate for a strike. As the ball came back, she could hear her Uncle Kaz's voice in her head. *Good hitters always strike at the balls they like. Throw it again.* And she did, for a second strike.

The boy at the plate wiggled his bat and pulled his face into a grimace.

Michiko threw a fastball, and he swung for the third time. *One down, two more to go*, she thought. But it wasn't to be. Before long, it was one man out and runners on second and third. Michiko pitched, and the batter hit a pop fly. She turned to see the runner on second heading for third. Bobby Wells caught the fly and faced third base. The runner turned and raced back to his base as Bobby swivelled and threw it to second. The smile on the runner's face collapsed when the second baseman tagged him.

The umpire called both the batter and the runner out. That double play had just put them back in the game! Now they had a chance.

It wasn't until Donald Maitland hit the ball right out of the park that they tied up the score, and it remained that way until the Bobby Wells gave them the lead by one. All the Braves had to do was make sure the other team didn't score. And they didn't.

Everyone on Michiko's team tossed their hats in the air to celebrate the Bronte Braves baseball team's first win. But as soon as Michiko's pigtails fell to her shoulders, she realized her mistake. *No one will notice,* she thought as she piled them back on top of her head and rammed on her hat. But the players in the field noticed, the players on the bench noticed, and the kids in the stands noticed.

Billy's face turned to ash.

"Their pitcher is a girl?" she heard someone yell in astonishment.

"We got some sort of confusion here," the other coach called out. "Girls playing on a boys' team? Isn't there some kind of rule about that?"

"Son of a gun," Coach Ward said. "She sure doesn't pitch like a girl." He shrugged and then gathered the team to go over what he liked about their game and what he didn't. Michiko almost forgot about taking off her hat until she and Billy walked to the parking lot. Everyone looked at her as if they had just seen a ghost.

The next day, Michiko and Mary walked past the group of boys that stood with their backs to the school wall. Usually the boys whistled or whispered behind their hands when they passed. Michiko knew it was Mary they all liked, but this time it was different.

"Is that the girl pitcher?" she heard one of them ask.

"Nah," another said, "that's just a rumour. Girls are no good at baseball."

"I heard she doesn't throw like a girl," another commented. "Someone said she's got an arm like Lefty Grove."

"A girl with an arm? No way, who says?"

"Eddie Adams."

"No kidding, who would have thought."

Mary looked at Michiko in surprise.

Carolyn and Mark approached Billy as they walked to the bus.

Mark put his face in front of Billy's. "She has to quit," he said. "Or none of the other teams will play us."

Billy backed up. "Maybe *you* should quit. That might make the team even better."

"Maybe both of you should quit," Mark said.

"Wanna make me?" Billy asked as he put up his fists.

The boys squared off like boxers.

"Fight, fight," resounded across the playground as a crowd formed a circle around them.

Billy launched himself at Mark and sent him to the ground. Mark jumped up with his fists flying, and this time Billy went down. Michiko put her hand to her mouth at the sight of blood flowing from his nose.

Out of nowhere the coach grabbed Mark by the collar. "You both want to get thrown off the team?" he asked. "Fighting is a good way to make it happen."

"Billy started it," Carolyn said as the coach marched the two boys away.

Michiko followed Annie onto the bus. She was going to have to quit playing baseball. It was already causing too much trouble for everyone.

Chapter 20

NO GIRLS ALLOWED

"You look lovely," the saleslady said as Michiko stepped out of the change room.

Michiko modelled the navy blue dress with fitted sleeves that her aunt had picked out. Other than a white scalloped collar, it was plain. And the waist seemed to be in the wrong place; in fact, there were two waists, one halfway up her chest.

The saleswoman turned to Sadie. "You were right," she said, "it is a good choice."

Sadie smiled. "I know my dresses," she said, indicating with her finger that Michiko was to turn around. "The wide band draws attention to your slim waistline."

"I look like a stick," Michiko said. "I want a full skirt and puffed sleeves."

"No, you don't," Sadie chided. "You want something timeless."

Michiko looked at the ceiling and rolled her eyes. *"What is time?"* her grandfather would say. He'd expect her to answer with mountains, oceans, and pine trees and nod in approval. *"But what about baseball?"* she'd once asked. *"Baseball is seasonal sport,"* he had replied with a grin, *"not much time to be wasted."*

"Growing up is taking too much time," Michiko complained.

"Time will always be on your side," Sadie responded, giving a wink to the saleslady. "You just watch. The most popular girl in the class will end up fat while you stay beautiful."

Michiko giggled at the thought of Carolyn growing fat. The saleslady gave her a big smile.

"Can I wear silk stockings?" Michiko asked with a knowing grin.

Sadie looked at her niece's feet. "I can see I'll have to buy you something decent for your feet, or you'll wear those baseball shoes." She turned to the saleslady. "We'll take the dress."

Michiko didn't have the heart to tell her aunt she needn't worry about her baseball shoes. She was thinking of hanging them up.

"The last time I bought you a dress was for Easter a long time ago," her aunt said as they waited for the dress to be boxed. "You were so cute with a big pink ribbon in your hair."

Michiko vaguely remembered painting hard-boiled eggs.

"Everyone stopped doing all that when the war

broke out," Sadie said to the saleswoman as she handed her the money.

The woman nodded as she passed Sadie the large white box.

Both Michiko and Sadie were surprised to see Mrs. Takahashi sitting in the living room when they arrived home. On her lap lay the small bundle of Geechan's letters and a notebook.

Her mother entered, carrying a tea tray.

After the correct introductions, Michiko watched her mother's guest slurp her tea. When she had drained her cup and eaten the last *mochi* from the plate, she sat back in the armchair and gave a sigh of contentment. "Now we can talk business," she said.

"You finished translating the letters?" Michiko asked.

Mrs. Takahashi looked down at her lap as if surprised to see them. "Your mother was right," she said. "They weren't very interesting. A lot of nonsense about people growing up together. But here they are." She picked them up and handed them and the notebook to Michiko. "That is only part of my business here today."

"What other business do you have?" Eiko asked. She looked at Sadie and Michiko on the couch, but Sadie just shrugged.

"It's all over town that the Japanese girl from the gladiola farm is playing baseball with the boys," Mrs. Takahashi said. "It's time to put a stop to such a ridiculous rumour."

Sadie's eyes narrowed. "What makes you think it is a rumour?"

"Because," Mrs. Takahashi said, taking a deep breath and raising her chin, "having a girl that acts like a boy is nothing to be proud of, and from what I know of your sister, she is a proud, traditional woman."

No one spoke for a moment. Michiko rose from her chair to leave, but Sadie pressed her arm, insisting that she stay. Out of the corner of her eye Michiko stole a glance at the woman's snub nose that always seemed to be looking down on others.

Eiko sat back in her chair and gave a small sigh. "I *am* a proud woman," she said. "I am proud of my heritage, my home, and my family."

Michiko lowered her eyes. She had never thought for a moment that playing baseball would be a slight against her family. As if they hadn't had enough problems from the war. Her eyes filled with tears as the thought of the humiliation she must have brought to her mother.

"We were not all that surprised Michiko made the baseball team," her mother continued.

Michiko looked up when her mother's voice dropped to a low murmur.

"Her father was sought after to play for the Asahi team," Eiko explained. Michiko noticed her mother's hands gripping the arms of the chair and her knuckles whitening. "He chose his responsibilities to his family and his job over the game."

Mrs. Takahashi nodded approvingly.

"You know," Michiko's mother continued, "I think a lot of people live their life backward. They think they choose the life they want, but they usually choose the life they fear."

Mrs. Takahashi furrowed her thin, pencilled brows.

Michiko glanced at Sadie, surprised to see that the colour had drained from her face.

"My daughter, you see, fears nothing," Eiko continued. "She isn't even afraid to get hit in the face by a hard ball." She gave Michiko a tender look. "We are very proud of the fact that she made the team. My husband does his best to attend all the games."

Mrs. Takahashi frowned. "You do know this will not help her in later life. Does she not know how to sew? Sewing is part of the basic preparation for marriage for all young women." She looked at Michiko and said, "For centuries, no matter how humble your home, you knew how to sew a kimono. When our grandmothers were girls, they started with raw silk, made the thread, wove the cloth, and dyed it."

"I can knit," Michiko replied in a tiny voice, but stopped as Sadie pressed her arm again. She looked at her mother. Eiko's glance was so scalding that she held her breath.

Her mother rose. "You have taken the time to translate my father's letters, for which we are grateful," she said, "but you needn't take any more of your time to translate our lives." She turned to Michiko. "You have homework, I believe," and then she said to Sadie, "Please see our guest to the door. I have to return to the big house."

Mrs. Takahashi rose and straightened her dress. "I can see myself out," she said. Then she walked over to Michiko and cupped her chin with her hand. "Young men don't marry girls who do not act like girls," she said, and then she left the room.

Michiko collapsed onto the couch, surprised at Mrs. Takahashi's words but even more surprised by her mother's support. It was usually Sadie who stuck up for her, but she had been the quiet one this time.

Why, Michiko wondered, *is everyone making kid business their business?*

The Braves' second game was against the team from Applegate Collegiate. Michiko felt uneasy now that everyone knew the pitcher for the Bronte Braves was a girl.

The Applegate Arrows warmed up in white tunics and caps with school crests.

She admired the school's manicured baseball field with its canvas bases. The first two rows of the glossy black bleachers had cushioned seats.

"Nice place," Michiko commented.

"I hate playing here," Billy said, "but there aren't enough teams to make a competition, so they gotta be part of ours. And they usually win every year."

At first there were just whispers when she walked by.

One of the Applegate Arrows waited at her team's bench with a cloth. His small, mean eyes squinted at her before he pretended to scour it clean. "Can't have a dirty bench," he said with a tight grin. "Girls don't like to get dirty."

Even the boys on her own team laughed.

In her head, Michiko knew she had to ignore it, but in her heart, it hurt.

The Applegate pitcher threw his glove down when Michiko stepped up to the plate. "I'm not playing against a girl," he shouted.

Their coach pulled him aside. After a short talk the pitcher returned to the mound, but his no-nonsense stare told her she was not welcome. He lobbed the ball, and it fell short of the plate. The second pitch was the same.

Michiko lowered her bat and tapped the base to let him know where it was.

When he threw the third ball, she moved forward in an effort to get a hit, swung, and missed. *Stupid*, she said to herself, seeing the pitcher sneer.

He lobbed the ball again, and she swung. Her bat caught the ball with the tip, and it flew upward and came down right into the shortstop's mitt.

"Yerrrr … out," the umpire called.

The pitcher threw his arms around his waist and doubled over with fake laughter.

Michiko dropped the bat and headed for the bench. *What am I doing?* she asked herself. She plunked herself down on the bench and put her head in her hands. *I should have let him walk me. At least I would have been on first.*

She pulled off her cap and shook her head to let her dark, shiny, pigtails fall to her shoulders. "I should have done that long ago," she said loudly. "It makes my head so much cooler."

"Don't you think she's got her diamonds all mixed up?" a voice called out from the crowd. A group of girls laughed. Michiko knew the voice immediately without having to look. Carolyn sat with her friends in the stands.

The next time she was up at the plate, the pitcher lobbed the ball to her again.

"Let it come to you," Coach Ward yelled. "Stay at the plate."

The third and fourth pitches fell short and Michiko walked. As she headed to first, the pitcher turned to her and bowed. "I didn't want to *hurt* you," he said. "My mother taught me never to play rough with girls."

The boys on his team bench laughed and thumped their thighs.

"A run is a run, even if you walk on it," Michiko said to the first baseman after she touched the base. "Your pitcher just loaded the bases." She turned to see the other team's coach approach the mound.

It only took one hit from Bobby Wells to bring all three of them in.

At the end of the fourth inning, Michiko could tell the other team's pitcher was getting tired by the way he dropped his arm at the end of a pitch and started missing the strike zone. She leaned over and whispered to Mark McAndrew, the boy next to her. "You're up next, you gotta bunt."

Mark, the catcher for their team, looked at her with disdain. "What would you know about bunting?"

"The pitcher's too tired to run up for the ball. It's a good idea."

Mark turned away from her and went to the plate.

The pitcher tossed the ball. Mark swung and missed. "Strike one," the umpire called.

Mark frowned at Michiko over his bat. She nodded vigorously to let him know he was to bunt.

Mark shrugged and positioned himself again. He missed for a second time.

The pitcher gave a huge stretch and yawned. He positioned himself and sent the ball Mark's way. Mark struck out.

But they won the game. And according to Billy, that had never happened before against Applegate.

As the players left the field, a tall man in a blue suit and fedora walked up to Coach Ward and took him to one side. The two of them walked about the field, talking. To Michiko's astonishment, when the man left, Coach Ward returned to the team and pointed at her.

"Can't use that lefty mitt at the next game," he said. "Come prepared or don't play."

Somehow Michiko knew it had nothing to do with owning a mitt; it had something to do with that man. Her throat squeezed shut as a feeling of sadness brimmed up inside her. She had to hold her breath to stop herself from crying as she left the field.

Chapter 21

THE BIRTHDAY PARTY

Michiko smoothed the front of her dress and took a deep breath before knocking at the Adams's front door. A trim, blond woman answered. Her pale skin shone like the several strands of pearls that filled the neckline of her soft, pink wool dress. She looked like she had just stepped out of an oyster shell. When the woman smiled, Michiko knew immediately she was Mary's mother.

"Isn't that a pretty dress," Mrs. Adams said to Michiko as she extended a hand adorned with an enormous sapphire in a heavy gold setting.

Michiko followed Mrs. Adams into the large front hall filled with the smell of waxed floors and fresh flowers. She looked down to admire the thin white straps that crossed her ankles as she walked across the dark Persian carpet. The white leather rose on the toe of her shoes made her feet so unbelievably beautiful, she felt like dancing.

They passed a door that opened into a room filled with books. Michiko could see a desk with a big black typewriter. She guessed the wide set of stairs with oak banisters led to the bedrooms on the second floor, but Michiko knew she wasn't to go up. Mrs. Adams led her into a large living room with a "Happy Birthday" banner hanging across its great stone fireplace.

"Mary will be down in a minute," Mrs. Adams said. "One of the girls is helping her dress. Please have a seat."

"That girl has no class," Carolyn said as she came down the stairs. "Your mother just invited her just to wind up the record player." She entered the room wearing a splashy print dress with heart-shaped pockets. At the sight of Michiko in her new dress and shoes, Carolyn opened her mouth in surprise. She had applied lipstick, but it was smeared across her teeth. "I saw that dress …" she said. Then she held her right wrist up and twisted it back and forth to make sure Michiko would see her crowded charm bracelet.

The room soon filled with other girls, many of whom did not go to Bronte Public School. Sadie had been right about the dresses. Even though the girls wore dresses of different materials with different collars, they all had short, puffed sleeves and full skirts.

Mary introduced Michiko to the girls in her French and dance classes. She met members of the 4-H club and daughters of Mary's mother's friends. All of them slid their eyes over her dress but went on talking about summer yachting parties and dinners at the Paradise Park Hotel.

"Do you have a boat?" one of the girls finally asked.

"I used to," Michiko replied. She smiled at the thought of the fishing expeditions she used to have with Clarence and Kiko.

"Sail or a motor?" another girl asked.

"Just oars," Michiko said, but the surprised look on their faces made her wish she hadn't.

"A rowboat?" the girl shrieked, while others in the group covered their mouths in amusement.

Mary's mother opened the doors to the dining room. She beckoned her daughter's guests to a large, lace-covered table set with platters of cold cuts rolled like cigars and festooned with parsley and radish roses. There was a red jelly salad, snow-white potato salad, and a tray of celery, pickles, and tiny white onions. There were also platters of heart-shaped cookies and beige, gooey squares.

As Michiko lifted a plate from the buffet, Eddie appeared at her side in a suit and tie. It was the first time she had seen him in anything other than blue jeans and a T-shirt. His dimpled grin and gleaming hair made him look like a film star. But by the way he tugged at his collar and sleeves, she could tell he wasn't comfortable.

"You look very nice," he said.

"So do you," she said, picking up a silver fork that was so heavy, it slipped out of her fingers. Her face went red at her clumsiness.

Eddie kicked the fork under the table and indicated she was to take another. When she took a seat on the sofa to eat, he perched on the arm beside her.

"You sure are different from my sister's other

friends," Eddie said through a mouthful of potato salad. "And you really know how to play ball."

"I wish I'd never tried out," Michiko muttered.

"Why?" Eddie asked. "Not everyone makes the team."

Michiko could see Carolyn watching them from across the room. Her voice dropped. "The coach just needed me to make up the numbers," she said. "He said so himself."

"Nah," Eddie said, putting his empty plate on the floor. "It's not the coach striking out the other players. You got a good arm."

Michiko pushed the rest of her food around her plate. "No one wants me to play."

"Who doesn't?"

She felt her throat tighten. The last thing she wanted to do was burst into tears in front everyone, especially Eddie. She paused. "I think someone complained about me being a girl."

"Wait a minute," Eddie said. He looked about the room. "I saw something the other day I knew would interest you." He reached out to the polished wood table at the side of the couch and lifted a magazine. Michiko recognized it as one they used to sell in their drug store. He passed it to her behind his back and whispered. "Check out the sports section on page ..." but stopped speaking as the lights flickered. Mary's mother stood in the doorway with a lighted birthday cake. Everyone stood to sing as the circle of light wavered across the ceiling.

While Mrs. Adams cut the cake, Michiko went into the hall to flip through the magazine. She stopped at the black and white pictures of young women playing baseball.

BASEBALL PITCHES IN FOR THE WAR EFFORT

Since the professional baseball players have traded their bats for bullets, The All American Girls Professional Baseball League has stepped up to the plate. The spring season for the Rockford Peaches, Fort Wayne Daisies, South Bend Blue Sox, Kenosha Comets, Grand Rapids Chicks, and the Racine Belles has started.

Michiko stared at the photograph of a young woman in a short-sleeved, belted tunic sliding into third base. Then she read on.

The All American Girls Professional Baseball League is the brainchild of Philip K. Wrigley, the chewing-gum millionaire who owns the Chicago Cubs. Annabelle Lee, Faye Dancer, and Mary "Bonnie" Baker are just a few of the girls in pigtails who perform dirt-churning slides. They're all confident their hair won't get in the way of a home run.

Michiko sat on the staircase to finish reading the article.

"You're just ahead of your time," Eddie said, coming to her side with a slice of cake on a plate. "People have to get used to women in sports," he said as he held out the plate. "Especially when they are as good as you."

"I still don't have a glove," Michiko said, putting the magazine on the stairs. "The coach said I had to have a decent glove or not to bother coming back."

"Then we better get you one," he said.

"Get one what?" Carolyn asked from behind. She leaned against the doorway of the dining room eating a piece of Mary's birthday cake.

"It's none of your business," Eddie said as he brushed past Michiko and ran up the stairs.

"Yes, it is," Carolyn said with a smirk as she took little bites of the cake.

But the crooked smile on her face faded when she saw Eddie come back down the stairs in blue jeans and a T-shirt, carrying a glove.

He held it out to Michiko.

Michiko's hands shook as she accepted it. "For me?"

"It's just sitting around in the closet," Eddie said. "I got a new one, remember?"

Michiko brought the glove to her face, closed her eyes, and inhaled the smell of oiled leather. "I'll take good care of it," she said in a low voice.

"I know you will," Eddie said. "And even though you look very pretty, you can't go to a practice dressed like that. I'll drive you home, and you can change."

Michiko thanked Mary and her mother for the lovely party.

"It's always nice to have a house full of young ladies," Mrs. Adams replied.

"Girls who swat at balls and whizz around on a bicycle are not ladies," Carolyn said in a low voice as she followed Michiko to the front porch. When Michiko got into the car, Carolyn hummed a few bars of "Row, Row, Row Your Boat."

Coach Ward showed up carrying a stack of apple baskets. "A couple at each base, on their sides," he called out as he tossed them to the players. He glanced in Michiko's direction and furrowed his brows. She held up Eddie's glove. He shrugged. "Let your eyes do the directing. One player at each base, to fish out the balls, the rest in the field. We're going to practise getting it to base."

He put Michiko on third base. She took a hard drive to the foot and hopped about.

"The boys are playing rough today," Billy said when she joined the line in the field.

Mark grinned. "You know what they say, if it's too hot, get out of the kitchen."

Michiko moved to the front of the line. She pulled the ball to her chest, took a deep breath, and fired it into the apple basket so hard, it went right through the bottom. Michiko hoped they now knew what it might feel like if she decided to drive a ball at someone's foot.

The unseasonal heat wave caused the boys to peel off their shirts and collapse on the grass at the end of practice. As Michiko lay in the shade by herself, she thought about the rock-filled lot that used to be their baseball diamond in the camp. Every ball bounced in a different direction when it hit the ground, and no one cared whether the players were girls or boys.

Chapter 22

IT'S OVER

After practice, Michiko picked up the mail from the box as usual. There was a letter from Kaz. She leaned her bike against the fence and sat by the side of the road to read it.

Dear Michiko,

These days I drink black coffee from china mugs an inch thick, but every coffee break comes with a couple of biscuits, which is a real treat.

A major visited and surprised us all when he spoke better Japanese than most of the recruits. He told us he was born in Japan and lived there until he was 19. He used to teach Japanese at Harvard University. All week long he tested our language. He told us how the graduates of the Japanese language school in Vancouver were serving in military positions.

Only a quarter of us were rated above average or excellent. I made the cut, which means I will be heading back to Vancouver. Next time you hear from me I'll be back in my old home town. If I can manage some leave, I'll be able to see Sadie.

Michiko nearly dropped the letter. They were sending Kaz back to Vancouver?

So happy to hear you made the team, and thanks for the information about Pete Gray. Some of the guys have tried some of his one-armed moves, and they are not easy.

She stuck the letter under her cap. *Kaz is going to look for Sadie. He won't be happy to find out she's not there.* But the new information gave her something to put in Johnny's next letter. Did she dare?

Even though the whole family had said their goodbyes before she'd gone to bed, Michiko rose at dawn to see her aunt before she returned to Toronto. She found Sadie standing by the front window. Her aunt's profile in the morning light reminded Michiko of one of those scissor portraits, facing one way, without a smile.

"Thanks again for the dress and shoes," Michiko whispered as she slid her arms around her aunt's waist. Sadie patted her head but said nothing.

Eiko entered the room carrying Hannah. "Such a grown-up name for such a little girl," Sadie murmured as she took the baby in her arms. Hannah's eyes shone, and she gave a smile of little pearly teeth. Michiko tickled her sister's pudgy toes.

Sadie's eyes filled with tears as she cuddled her. "When I moved to Toronto, I promised myself that I was finished talking about this stupid war. I fought injustice for three years, and it was time for me to pay attention to something else. So I focused on having an old-fashioned married life, and now that has been taken from me as well."

"You'll get it back," Eiko responded.

"*Itsu?*" Sadie asked.

"You just have to wait, like I did for Sam."

"I was a fool to burn Kaz's letter without even reading it," Sadie said in a low voice. "I don't even know where he is."

But I do, Michiko realized. She slipped into her bedroom and pulled Kaz's last letter from her little blue box.

Sadie stepped outside carrying Hannah. Eiko followed.

Michiko lifted the clasp of her aunt's purse and pushed the letter underneath her embroidered silk change purse. Snapping it shut, she called out, "Don't forget this," picked up the purse, and ran outside.

Later that morning, Michiko stood beside her mother watching her stir chopped cabbage into ground beef and add a dash of *shoyu*. Eiko placed a spoonful of the mixture into the centre of a small circle of dough. She lifted the bottom half of the wrap and pressed the edges together. "Pay attention," she said. "One day, you will be making dinner by yourself."

But Michiko didn't care about making *gyoza*. She wanted to learn how to make the crispy marshmallow treats that were at Mary's party. *Instead of getting to do what I want to do in the kitchen*, she thought, *I have to set the table and do the dishes*. To make matters worse, she knew if her mother had to ask her to do something more than once, she would end up sitting on the front porch and thinking about her responsibilities. Life was so unfair.

"Don't forget I've got a game today," Michiko said.

"Wash your hands," was all her mother said.

At least I think I have a game, Michiko thought. *Coach said nothing about the glove, even though Billy made a big fuss.* Her thoughts drifted to what the opposing team would be like this time.

"If we win this game," Billy said, walking out to the diamond, "it'll be three in a row."

"Always add caution to caution," Michiko said.

"What the heck is that supposed to mean?" Billy asked.

"It's something my grandfather always said to me when I was little," Michiko said.

"Sorta 'Don't count your chickens before they hatch?'" Billy asked. "That's what my grandpa is always saying to me."

"Don't worry," they overheard a boy from the other team say as they walked from the parking lot. "Girls are no good at baseball."

Michiko stopped in her tracks. Then she strode over to them with her hands on her hips. "Haven't you heard of Penny O'Brian, the Canadian playing professional baseball in the States?"

The boys stopped talking to look at her.

Out of the corner of her eye, Michiko saw the man in the blue suit, wearing his brimmed hat low on his brow, getting out of his car. Realizing it wasn't a good idea to draw attention, she turned away and joined her team.

The game against the Canning Factory Cardinals was an easy win. Their centre fielder kept on racing forward while the ball sailed over his head. The right fielder called the ball but kept on falling as he staggered backward, letting the ball drop to the grass. The left fielder fumbled the ball every time he caught it. The others also overshot the base on their throws.

The game ended with a score of 8–1 for the Braves.

"Those guys play just like girls," Mark commented as they headed toward their bikes. Michiko glared at him, but he didn't seem to notice.

"Why are you so interested in all this, Leahey?" Michiko and Billy heard Coach Ward ask the man in the blue suit. The two of them stood face to face in front of the coach's car. "You don't even have a son."

Michiko and Billy turned to each other. *That man is Carolyn's father?*

"It's the principle of the thing," Mr. Leahey replied.

"What principle?"

"Girls don't belong on a baseball field. It's not ladylike."

"So," the coach said, heaving his large belly up over his belt, "let me get this straight. It's okay for women to hold down jobs in factories, drive ambulances, and put out fires while this war is on, but not all right for girls to play baseball in a small town junior league."

The man removed his hat and looked around the field.

"Is that what you are saying?" the coach asked, much louder.

The rest of the Bronte Braves gathered around to listen.

"Obviously you don't pay any attention to regulations," Mr. Leahey said. "Perhaps you have no business coaching this team."

One of the boys on the team murmured, "We don't need a girl on our team."

"She can pitch better than you," Billy said, giving him a shove.

The man laughed. "She lied about being a boy," he said, putting his hat back on. "You don't want a liar on your team, do you?"

Michiko couldn't take it any longer. Everyone stood there talking about her as if she didn't exist, and Mr. Leahey had just called her a liar. She pushed her way through the boys and stood between the coach and Carolyn's father.

"Mitch is short for Michiko," she said, putting her hand on her hips, "my Japanese name." She felt her face getting red. "No one asked me if I was a girl at tryouts, and I NEVER ONCE said I was a boy."

Both the coach and Mr. Leahey took a step back.

Michiko remembered something her father once said. "Maybe," she said, turning to Coach Ward, "it's time everyone stopped paying attention to the length of my hair and started looking at my earned run average? Do you want to win or not?"

Coach Ward looked at her in surprise, and a huge grin broke out across his face. "You've got spunk," he said. "I'll give you that."

He scratched his chin for a moment while Mr. Leahey shifted from one foot to the other. Then he turned to Carolyn's father. "She's right, with her on the team we have a good chance of winning. You'd think you'd be proud of your home team, instead of making trouble for them."

"*My* home team?" the man said. His voice twisted with unmistakeable sarcasm. "This bunch of farmers and fruit pickers is not *my* team. I attended Applegate College." He turned on his heel and stormed off.

"Your real name is Michiko?" Billy asked as they walked to their bikes. "Why does the teacher call you Millie?"

"Long story," Michiko said, shaking her head.

"What do you want me to call you?"

"Whatever you want," she replied, too weary to talk.

Mr. Nott appeared in the doorway of their classroom the next morning. "All senior students will assemble in the gymnasium," he said in a serious voice and moved across the hall.

Michiko's class followed their teacher out of the door, merging with the others to form a noisy, expectant crowd.

"I bet there's going to be an air raid," one of the boys called out.

"I bet the Germans invaded Britain," said another.

Mary reached for Michiko's fingers and gave them a squeeze. She looked pale.

The principal strode to the podium and held up his hand for silence. They waited in the large room that smelled like dirty socks and rubber balls, facing the stage, wondering what was about to happen. He surveyed the students for a moment and then spoke. "Germany has surrendered," he said. "The war in Europe is over."

No one said anything at first, turning to look at the person beside them in disbelief.

"Did he just say what I think he said?" Mary asked.

"Senior students are to be given the rest of the day off," the principal announced, and with that the gymnasium erupted into a great noise of cheering and yelling. Several teachers came to the front, singing "God Save the King" at the top of their voices.

The students surged out of the auditorium on to the front lawn to the sound of church bells ringing and the continual blast of the basket factory whistle. Like a swarm of bees, they made their way down to the village main street, laughing and cheering. The man who owned the drugstore lit firecrackers. Men appeared on the roof of the hardware store waving flags. There were all kinds of people coming out of buildings and cars, yelling and singing at the top of their voices.

Eddie waved to Michiko as he took his sister's hand.

"I better go back for Annie," Billy said to Michiko, when the rest of the students had dispersed into the crowd.

Michiko followed him to the school bus. Their driver sang as he drove past the cars that moved up and down the road, honking. They passed a truck with a huge sheet across the back, painted with the words NAZIS SURRENDER and flapping in the breeze. Their driver took off his hat and tossed it out the window. Everyone on the bus cheered.

Her mother was putting sheets on the line when Michiko arrived home. Michiko watched her pull clothespins from the deep front pocket of her apron and clip them to the edge. She drew another damp sheet from the basket and fixed it to the line.

Mrs. Palumbo walked past them toward the vegetable garden with an empty basket. She smelled of raw onions.

"You're home early," Eiko said. She looked at Michiko's sweaty face and unruly hair and furrowed her brows. "What have you been doing with yourself?" she asked. "You look as if you walked all the way home from school. Was there a problem with the bus?"

Before Michiko could explain being jostled by the jubilant crowd, the sound of church bells punctuated the quiet of the flower farm.

"Why are the church bells ringing?" her mother asked. A look of alarm crossed her face.

"It's over," Michiko said with a grin.

"What's over?"

Before Michiko could answer, Mr. Palumbo rushed past them into the vegetable garden.

"Cosa succede?" his wife asked, raising her head from the tomato plants.

Mr. Palumbo grabbed her by the hand and pulled her out onto the lawn.

She fought his attempts to put his arm about her waist until he whispered something in her ear. Then she threw back her head and shrieked. They broke apart. With her hands on her hips, Mrs. Palumbo kicked her feet back and forth, circling her husband. Then she threw her hands high above her head and clapped to create a rhythm.

Michiko knew her bewildered mother never listened to the news or read the newspapers, to avoid events. She took her by the hand and led her into the house.

Her father was in the kitchen. He had the volume up, and the voice of the news reporter blasted into the kitchen. "Canadians stormed the beaches of Normandy. Two thousand and seventy-six days after the start of the war, it is finally over. Germany has surrendered."

Her mother sank down into one of the kitchen chairs. "The war is over?" She pressed her fingers to her mouth. "It is really over?"

Sensing her mother's disbelief, Michiko put her hand on top of her mother's. "That's why we're home from school early," but she stopped speaking, surprised by her mother's trembling.

The next day they walked to St. John's Church under the cool avenue of elm trees along the road. Sam held Hiro's hand. Michiko and her mother followed with the baby buggy.

The minister stood at the door welcoming everyone as the bells rang out. "There are plenty of seats at the front," he said through a large grin.

The dim yellow light of the church's hanging chandeliers and wall sconces seemed unnecessary on such a sunny day. The congregation chatted amid the smell of candle wax and fresh flowers. Michiko was used to Japanese faces filling most of the pews in the small church of the ghost town. Here they had to walk past a sea of *hakujin* to get to the pews at the front.

The happy chatter of the congregation turned to quiet whispers when the members of the choir entered through a door behind the pulpit and settled in the choir stall. The minister took his place at the wooden podium and invited the choir to sing.

Michiko watched their *o*-shaped mouths and radiant faces but was irritated by the high-pitched voice of a woman refusing to blend with the others.

The minister rose from his wooden throne to speak.

"Today we come together to give thanks that the war is over, but with sadness at the thousands of men, women, and children who gave their lives to this great conflict," the minister said. "For them, there will be no jubilance, no celebrations, no three cheers for the King. But this is not a sad thing, for they have heard the clearest, most beautiful sound of all, the clarion call on high. They will have felt the greatest love of all."

There was not one whisper among the people.

The minister looked out over the crowd. "We will never forget the loss of those we loved, nor should we, but we must also focus our prayers on those who are still so very far away, the ones that have yet to get back home."

Michiko closed her eyes to do as the minister asked. *What about Gerald? Will he be able to get back to playing baseball? What about Francis and his leaky pen? Why is he taking so long to write back? What about Johnny?* She guessed her last letter had made him stop writing to her. And then she thought about Kaz and grinned. Her uncle wouldn't have to go off to fight after all.

"We must show great care and concern for those who arrive back on Canadian shores," the minister was saying, "not just because they may have been wounded or seen things that do not bear repeating. When we care deeply about someone else; we put a new kind of energy into the world. And we need this new kind of energy in a very great way. Other people will pick it up and make themselves better people. This is called giving Grace, and this is what I mean when I say to you, 'Go with God's Grace.'"

The choir stood to sing again. Michiko decided to think nice thoughts about the woman with the out-of-tune voice. She smiled at her, and to her surprise the woman smiled back.

Everyone milled about the front of the church, smiling and shaking hands as the bells rang and rang. Michiko thought it was the happiest day of her life until someone grabbed her elbow and hissed in her ear. "We are still at war with the Japs," Carolyn said in a low voice.

My war will never be over, Michiko thought as they made their way home.

That night Michiko watched her father eat his dinner. He used his chopsticks with such skill, he always began his meal with the smallest pieces on his plate, unlike her brother, who searched for the largest and crammed it into his mouth.

"Sadie's got a nice place," he said to her mother at the end of the meal. "She's on a street of houses full of Japanese people. Many of them were teachers at the schools in camps."

"Auntie Sadie has a house?" Michiko asked.

"She rents a room," Sam said. "She'll get a house the same way we will, by saving."

"It's different now," Eiko said. "People get mortgages."

"Japanese people don't borrow money," Sam said. "You said that yourself."

"That was before the war," Eiko said.

"My animals have a house," Hiro said. He sat on the kitchen floor with his Noah's ark animals, making each pair walk up the painted plank to the deck of the wide wooden boat. Another two would arrive in the mail, any day now, just in time for his birthday. Just like her father, Uncle Ted never failed to surprise them with his amazing woodworking talents.

"Your animals live in a boat," Michiko said. The memory of the girls' reaction to her uncle's rowboat at Mary's party made her face burn red. *I wish we could move to Toronto and live on a street full of Japanese people.*

Chapter 23

STRAWBERRIES

The heat hung about the house like a blanket, but it was the excitement of the next day that had kept Michiko awake. Her first crop of strawberries was ready for harvest.

"The going rate is five cents a pint," Mr. Downey told her as he handed her a stack of new berry boxes and a jar with a slot in the lid. "You don't have to sit by the side of the road all day," he said. "Make a sign. People will take what they need if you aren't there and leave the money in the jar. Just make sure you collect the money and refill the table on a regular basis."

Her mother supervised Michiko's first harvest of the small, bumpy berries, "No one wants their strawberries to be in a condition ready for jam," she said as she demonstrated how to look under the leaves for the deep crimson berries and gently loosen them from their stems. Then Eiko left the strawberry patch and went back to her work. She lifted a pillowcase from her laundry basket, snapped it, and clipped it to the line. She yanked the rope, making the pulley squeal, and then hung the next one. Michiko picked berry after berry as her mother pegged out the sheets.

Mrs. Palumbo joined Michiko in the garden. "Dat Hitler," she said as she reached out and snapped off a stalk of asparagus. "Dat's what I like to do to him." She stared at the spiked spear and spat on the ground.

Michiko lowered her eyes. Sometimes Mrs. Palumbo displayed a vehemence that frightened her. Her mother once told her Mrs. Palumbo believed that restraint was harmful to her health and would hurl insults at anyone until she felt better. Michiko moved out of the old woman's spitting range, put her head down, and kept on picking.

That afternoon, after nailing up her sign, Michiko planted her elbows on the tabletop of the wooden stall her father had built. She was thankful for the shade the tiny, shingled roof provided. Like everything her father made, the edges were precise and the surfaces smooth. Settling her face into her hands, she released a long sigh. It took a lot more work than she thought it would to fill six pint boxes.

Mrs. Morrison, the cat, wound her way through Michiko's legs. Then she extended her front paws along the ground in front of her and offered up her backside for scratching. "Make sure you stay off the road," Michiko said as the cat arched its back and stuck its tail straight up in the air when she petted it. "We don't want you to get hit by a car."

Her first customer was a woman with white hair whose gold-rimmed glasses sat birdlike on her small pointed nose. She took a box of strawberries into her fine-boned bird hands and examined it. "Are they all ripe?" she asked. "No white ones on the bottom?"

Michiko nodded. "I picked each one myself."

The woman put down the box and unzipped her change purse. But before she could extract any money, a man got out of the car and appeared at her side.

"We're not buying anything off the Japs," he said angrily.

"But they don't own the farm," the woman protested.

"Then the owner is a sympathizer," he said, tugging at her elbow.

The woman gave out a deep sigh and pushed the box toward Michiko.

"Those Japs killed my neighbour's brother," he said loudly. He looked back at her as he steered the woman away. "Why don't you Nips all go back where you came from."

Michiko's throat constricted and her chest went tight as the man and woman drove away with tires squealing.

It wasn't one of us, she wanted to call out as a truck pulled up in front of her.

A scrawny, sunburned young woman in a faded housedress got out from the passenger side. She pushed back wisps of hair escaping from the pile on top of her head held together with grip pins and asked, "Are any of them cheaper because they're crushed?"

Michiko shook her head. She had lost the desire to talk.

The woman got back in the truck without buying and drove off.

When the next vehicle slowed down, the beige soft top told her it was a convertible. The green car pulled into Billy's laneway. Michiko stood up in disbelief.

Carolyn got out and waved at her from across the road. The car drove on down the lane to Billy's house as Carolyn crossed the road.

Michiko picked up the jar of money and stuffed it into the front pocket of her overalls.

"These look good," Carolyn said, picking a few strawberries from the box in front of her and popping them into her mouth. "Mmmm," she said licking her lips, "they are really good."

This time she took a handful of berries from the box.

Michiko moved the box away from her. "They are not free," she said.

"I'll get the money from my dad when he comes back," she said, reaching out for more.

The last thing Michiko needed was Carolyn eating her out of business. She pulled the remaining boxes into her arms. "I'm closing up shop," she said. "Come back when you have money."

Carolyn licked her fingers one at a time. "That's okay," she said. "I told my dad I would stay with you until he was finished talking to Billy's dad."

Michiko ignored her and walked toward the house.

"MILLIE," Carolyn yelled as she moved into the laneway.

Michiko turned back to see what she wanted.

Carolyn had a small rubber ball in her hand. "Catch," she said, throwing the ball.

Michiko turned to avoid the impossible, but the ball hit her hard in the arm, and she dropped the berry baskets into the dust.

"You knew I couldn't catch it," Michiko shrieked. "My hands were full of strawberries."

"I wanted to see you make one of your famous plays," Carolyn said with a smirk. Strawberries scattered the road like red raindrops. Michiko crouched to upright the containers. "They're all dirty," she said.

"I'll help you," Carolyn said.

Michiko didn't look up until a white majorette boot came down on top of one of the thin wooden containers. It collapsed.

"Oops," Carolyn said, lifting her boot and scraping it on the grass. "I didn't see it."

Michiko had to moisten her lips with the tip of her tongue before she could talk. "Yes, you did," she said. "You did that on purpose, just like you threw …" but she stopped talking as her throat tightened and her anger rose. She reached for a handful of the strawberries lying in the dirt, and threw them. The crushed red berries landed on the starched lace collar of Carolyn's white blouse and slid down the front, leaving a juicy red trail.

Carolyn looked down in shock. "Look what you've done," she said, staring at the damp red lines down the front of her blouse. "My mother just bought me this blouse."

"You wanted to play catch," Michiko said. She gathered another handful of crushed berries and threw them in Carolyn's face.

"You are in big trouble, Jap girl," Carolyn sputtered. "I'm going to tell."

Michiko walked toward the house cradling the remaining fruit boxes in her arms. Her heart was pounding so hard, she thought it would explode.

Carolyn followed her down the lane with her hands on her hips and called out. "I'll get your father fired."

Michiko's eyes narrowed. As she reached the garden, Mrs. Palumbo stood to stretch her back, holding a handful of freshly pulled weeds. Her mother was nowhere in sight.

"See that girl," Michiko said to her in a low voice. The man's harsh words echoed in her mind. Mrs. Palumbo furrowed her brows and looked in the direction that Michiko pointed. "She just said that all Italians should go back to where they came from."

The old Italian woman turned slowly toward Carolyn. Her lips pulled pack into a snarl as she raised the handful of weeds.

"*Va!*" she screamed.

Carolyn's face blanched as she backed away from the terrifying old woman.

"*VA!*" Mrs. Palumbo screamed even louder as she moved forward. She spoke with such force, it was as if Mr. Downey's tractor was backfiring.

Carolyn turned and ran for her life.

Michiko looked around to see if anyone had witnessed what had just happened, and then she opened the gate and bent to pick more strawberries. Her heart was full of fear. *Carolyn can't really get my father fired? Can she?*

Mrs. Palumbo returned to the garden, muttering words Michiko didn't understand. Michiko felt a pang of regret for involving the old woman. *What if Mr. Palumbo gets fired as well?* She picked strawberries until her mother called her for dinner.

That evening, while drying the dishes, Michiko was struck by the most terrifying thought of all. *Why was Mr. Leahey visiting Billy's father? Is he going to get Billy's dad to speak to my dad about getting me off the team?* Her stomach sank.

Michiko slid out from under her sheets just as the low rumblings in the sky turned to rushing rain. She jumped at the flash of lightning that filled her bedroom with light. The next flash brought a large crack of thunder that seemed to split the house in half. Hiro's bare feet raced down the hall and into her parents' room.

This is good, Michiko thought as she made her way to the bathroom. Their game would be cancelled, and she wouldn't have to worry about whether to show up or not. Lightning lit up the entire back field. She could see the trenches her father had dug for the corms running like tiny rivers. Someone approached the Palumbos' house with collar turned up and hands burrowed into the pockets of an overcoat. Michiko waited by the window to watch.

The front door of the neighbour's house flew open. Mrs. Palumbo, in a dressing gown with her grey hair in a long braid down the side of her shoulder, pulled the person inside.

Michiko slipped back under her covers, listening to the heavy patter against the roof, wondering what was going on in the house next door.

Chapter 24

ANTONIO

Michiko always held Hiro's hand when they went up to the road, but this morning he broke away from her and began to run. "Hiro," she called out, "you're supposed to walk with me." She sighed at the thought of having to chase him down. But before he made it past the big house, someone scooped him up.

"Where are you going, little guy?" a deep voice asked.

"Who are you?" Michiko asked the young man. He wore a new houndstooth jacket over trousers with a sharp crease. It was clear he had spent many minutes polishing his black leather shoes. His wild, curly black hair flopped over a pair of horn-rimmed sunglasses.

"I'm Antonio Palumbo," he said, "but everyone calls me Tony. Those shoes look pretty good on you. They're mine, you know."

"But …" Michiko sputtered.

"I'm just pulling your leg," the young man said. "I grew out of them long ago. Good thing for you Mamma kept them."

To Hiro's great delight, Tony hoisted the little boy onto his shoulders. "My father used to lift me on to his shoulders when I was a kid," he said. "I thought I was king of the world being up so high. I could touch the branches of the tree and pick off some of the best apples."

"You couldn't have made him happier," Michiko said. "You'll have a friend for life."

"Where are you heading?"

"Just up to the mailbox," Michiko answered.

"You go," Tony said. "I'll keep him occupied."

One of the letters was addressed to her mother. Michiko could tell by the writing that it was from her Aunt Sadie. To Michiko's delight, the other one was from her uncle. She sat down on the grass and opened it.

Dear Michiko,

Just think after three years of being pushed out of Vancouver, I am back. When we reached the place where British Columbia begins, the train made a ten-minute stop. All of us got out to fill our lungs with fresh air. One of the guys with us couldn't wait to show us his father's strawberry farm in the Fraser Valley, but when we passed through it, he was really disappointed to see the fields full of hay. At the CPR station there were army officers on the platform. We were a bit nervous, but they were there to greet us and take roll call. They even had trucks waiting for us to take us to the school. It turns out the Allied Translator and Interpreter School is right beside the Vancouver Technical School. Tell your dad that, he'd know exactly where.

Michiko stopped reading. She hadn't told anyone she got letters from Kaz. There was no real reason to keep it secret; it just got so complicated, and she didn't want to get in trouble for not minding her own business. She stuffed it into her overalls to finish reading it in her room.

Hiro sat on the porch with his elbows on his knees and his head in his hands, staring at the ground. Tony sat beside him. Together they were watching a small green snake make its way through the grass.

Tony looked up. "My father told me you're pretty good at baseball."

Michiko shrugged. *He'll probably make fun of me for playing.*

"So when's your next game?"

Michiko gave a great sigh. "Tonight," she said. "If the ground's not too wet."

"Great," he said. "I'll be there to see it." He got up, dusted off his pants, and patted Hiro on the head.

"Why don't you live here anymore?" Michiko blurted out.

"Better money in Toronto," he said as he walked toward the lane.

Her father followed her into the house, but the air in the kitchen changed with the package he carried. Michiko's eyes began to water.

"What on earth is that smell?" Eiko cried out.

Sam pointed to the long, damp package he had put on the table. "*Okoko*," he said in protest. "It's a present from Mrs. Takahashi."

Eiko muffled her mouth with her apron to stop herself from gagging. She grabbed the package and threw it out the open window.

Michiko covered her nose with the tea towel but also covered her smile. Mrs. Takahashi had sent them the stinky yellow pickle that smells up Japanese households.

"You are not going to stink up the whole house for a few slivers of pickled turnip," her mother said, slamming the window shut. "If you want to eat it, keep it in the barn."

Sam went outside to retrieve the package.

Eiko muttered, "If there was trouble to be stirred, that woman would hold the spoon."

While making dinner, Michiko's mother spoke with great enthusiasm about Sadie's new job. "It looks as if her experience in the dress shop has paid off. She got a full-time job dressing the windows for a department store."

"That sounds like fun," Michiko said. She could just see her aunt adjusting the bodies, hands, and heads of the mannequins to create scenes that showed the latest fashions.

"She is also able to put her paper cutting skills to work," her mother said. "Apparently she filled the windows with wax clouds and raindrops and put everyone in raincoats. Lots of people in the street stopped to admire it."

"She'll make the windows beautiful," Michiko said, imagining windows full of the Japanese rain chains her aunt had taught her to make, "and she'll make lots of money."

"Why would you say that?"

"I met Antonio Palumbo today," Michiko said. "He makes lots of money in Toronto."

"People always make more money in the city," her mother replied as she waved her apron about the room. "They pay more for everything else as well."

Michiko found Tony sitting at the fruit stand when she went to replenish the berries.

"Old Mr. Downey must be doing well," he said. "How much is he charging for these?"

"Five cents a pint," Michiko replied. She hoped she wouldn't have to rescue this crop from free samples as well.

"Must be making money elsewhere to afford this fancy stand," he said. "When I sold them, all I had was an old kitchen chair, a wooden box, and an umbrella."

"My father built it," Michiko said as she lined up the boxes in a neat row. She looked up at the tiny roof and once again admired the perfectly laid shingles.

"You're kidding," Tony said.

"He made my sister's playpen, and he made me a cedar chest," she bragged.

"Can I see them?"

Michiko shrugged. It seemed strange that a grown man would want to look at a baby's playpen and a girl's hope chest. "Just ask my mom," she said.

It took less than an hour to sell her day's harvest, with two customers buying the whole lot. Michiko skipped down the lane to the house. Hannah had just learned to crawl, and she loved spending time on the floor with her. Whatever Michiko did, her sister laughed and clapped.

When she walked into the house, she could hear her father talking to someone. She found him and Antonio on their knees, examining her hope chest.

"Is there something wrong with it?" Michiko asked. She always thought her *tansu* was too plain. The grain and the colour of the wood were its only decoration. Even the clasp was simple.

"Everything is right with it," Tony said. "Your father should be making furniture instead of planting flowers."

Her father waved the compliment away. They put the chest back against the wall. "I don't have the tools I used to have in …" Sam paused, "Japan."

"Where I work, they have walls of tools. You can use anything you want, as long as they are all put back in the same place, clean."

Sam nodded in approval.

"Except me. They won't let *Eye-ties* in the workshop. They only let us deliver."

Sam patted the boy's back. "*Gaman suru,*" he said. "*Gaman suru.*"

Tony looked at Michiko. "What does that mean?"

Michiko rolled her eyes. "You have to be patient," she said.

"You'd think with this war over, they'd give people like us a chance," Tony said as he opened the kitchen door. "All I want to do is build furniture."

And all I want to do is play baseball, Michiko thought as she flopped down on the chair.

That evening, Michiko waited for Coach Ward to pull into the parking lot.

"You must be anxious to play," the coach said as unlocked the trunk.

"I'm not going to play," Michiko said. She kicked at the gravel with the toe of her shoe.

"You not feeling well?" the coach asked as he threw the duffle bag to the ground.

"I feel fine," Michiko said, although she really didn't. Her stomach churned. "You are going to make me quit anyway," she said. "I'm just saving you the trouble."

"Why would I want you to quit?" Coach Ward looked at her in amazement.

"It's in the regulations," Michiko said. "No girls allowed."

"I made it my business to read through all the regulations," Coach Ward said. "And there isn't one that says the team has to be all boys. The regulations just refer to the team, every time." He handed her the cloth bases to carry. "We need you Mitch, Millie, or whatever the heck your name is. You are the team's secret weapon."

"I am?"

"Sure," he said. "The boys who believe that girls are no good at sports are only fooling themselves. They might think playing against a girl is a joke. But the joke ends up on them."

Michiko jumped high, plucked the ball from the air, and fired it home. The entire team rose from the bench and cheered when the umpire called both the batter and the runner out. The next batter drove the ball so hard, when it hit her glove she went down on one knee. Michiko expected to see a hole as she stood up. *Throw it to second,* she thought, until she spotted the player on third running home. She spun and fired it, getting that runner out as well. The crowd went wild. She could hear Tony cheering louder than anyone else.

"You play better than I did when I was your age," he said at the end of the game.

"You gotta practice," Michiko said with a smile, "to be good at what you love to do."

"That's true," he said. He reached into his shirt pocket and pulled out a paper.

"See this," he said. "I'm going to apply for a job with another company."

Michiko studied the advertisement. A furniture factory in Toronto was advertising for experienced workers.

"Right now it's just a collection of garages that the guy rents in the courtyard of an old mansion," he explained. "He's asking everyone who wants a job to come with a wooden box that they made themselves."

He looked around and then whispered, "But don't tell my mother, she thinks I've come home to the farm to stay."

Michiko had witnessed Mrs. Palumbo's reaction to things she didn't like. "You have no idea how good I am at keeping secrets," she said. "I could be a spy. Can I keep this?"

Chapter 25

KAMIKAZE

The next morning, Michiko brought the blue box Clarence had made into the kitchen and put it down in front of her father.

"For me?" he said as he lowered his newspaper.

"I need a bigger box for my letters," Michiko said, "and Mr. Palumbo's son needs to learn how to build one."

Her father said nothing.

"I thought," Michiko continued with a shy smile, "that you could teach him by making me a new one, like my *tansu,* only smaller."

Her father took a long time to answer, so long that Michiko thought she would have to repeat her request, and then he put his finger to her forehead and said, "*maho.*"

Michiko looked to her mother for an explanation, but before she could speak, her father laughed out loud. "Now I know why you're so good at baseball," he said. "You read minds!"

"It's not magic," her mother said, placing her hand on Michiko's shoulder. "She is a kind person, and this is a kind thing for her to suggest."

Her father went back to his newspaper just as Hiro came into the kitchen, crying.

"Mrs. Morrison is gone," he said. "I looked everywhere."

Michiko glanced at the small dishes on the floor. Both were still full. "I'll bet she is up one of the trees," she said, pulling her little brother onto her lap, "like before."

Hiro shook his head. "She's gone."

"We'll find her," Michiko said. "Come with me."

Together, they searched the property. By lunchtime, Michiko was also concerned. She didn't want to check the road and decided to ask for help.

"What's up?" Tony asked when they approached the Palumbo house.

"My brother's cat is missing," Michiko told him. "Would you check the r-o-a-d?"

"Sure," he said. "I'll use the bike."

Tony came to their door just as they were finishing their lunch. "All clear," he said. "When did you see the cat last?"

Hiro stuck out his lower lip and shrugged.

"She followed me to the strawberry stand yesterday," Michiko said. "That's why I wanted you to check the road." She didn't like to think about the day Carolyn showed up, and then she felt her heart collapse like an umbrella as the most horrible of thoughts struck her.

Michiko turned to her little brother. "I think Mrs.

Morrison went to visit someone," she said. "Don't worry, we'll find her."

She lined the basket in front of her bicycle with a piece of worn cloth and set off down the lane toward the village. It wouldn't be too difficult to find Carolyn's house. She lived on the same street as Mary, and Michiko knew Mr. Leahey's car. It being Sunday, she hoped it would be in the driveway, and it was.

At first, Michiko planned to pound on the front door and demand that Carolyn give the cat back, but her resolve faded as she leaned her bike against one of the trees in the boulevard. It was only a hunch. She decided to look in the backyard and walked to the gate at the side of the large stone house and gave it a push. It swung open with a loud creak. Michiko held her breath as she followed the walkway calling out to the cat in a soft voice. Just as she searched a large flower garden, a voice from the back porch said, "You know that you're trespassing, don't you?"

Michiko straightened her back and turned to face Carolyn.

Carolyn rose from a garden chair wearing white shorts and shirt. She held a tennis racket.

Michiko stepped up to the porch. "If you took that cat," she said, " I will ... I will ..." She faltered, trying to think of a terrible fate. "I will *KAMIKAZE* you."

"Daddy," Carolyn called out in a shrill voice. "Daddy, I need you."

The back door to the house flew open and a woman appeared. "Your father is on the phone," she said in an irritated manner. "What's the matter now?"

"There's a strange girl in our backyard," Carolyn cried out. "She's threatening to hurt me."

The woman stepped out on to the porch.

"Hello, Mrs. Leahey," Michikó said in her most polite voice. "I'm in Carolyn's class at school. I guess she couldn't tell because the sun was in her eyes."

The woman took a step closer to get a better look at Michiko. She looked at Carolyn and then at Michiko. "Why are you in our backyard?

"I was looking for my brother's cat," Michiko replied. She looked directly at Carolyn and said, "I thought she might have gotten into your yard by accident."

"Your cat?" the woman said. "Carolyn said it was a stray. I'm allergic to cats, so she took it to the pound. It's not far from here."

Michiko thanked her and went toward the gate. Just as she lifted the latch, she heard a plaintive mew. It came from the garden shed at the back of the property.

Carolyn ran to the shed, but Michiko got to it first and opened the door. "Here, kitty, kitty," she called in a soft voice.

Mrs. Morrison, the black and white cat with its distinctive milk drop marking, came toward her, mewing softly. She looked scared. Michiko picked her up, took a deep breath, and turned to face Carolyn.

"How could you steal a little boy's cat?" she asked. "How could anyone be so mean?"

Carolyn gave a shrug, but her smirk faded as her mother approached. "You told me you took that cat to the pound," she said.

Michiko unlatched the gate with one hand, cradling the cat with the other. "Carolyn says a lot of things, Mrs. Leahey," she said, "most of which are not true." Then she ran to her bike, placed the cat in the basket, and pedalled away.

The fielder for the Seaway Seagulls ran for the ball, but not knowing whether to throw it to first or home, hesitated and threw it home. The catcher had expected a throw to first and was not at the plate. The ball dropped and rolled toward the pitcher's mound. The pitcher scrambled to pick it up, but Michiko, who was on third, made it to the home plate, winning the game 7–6.

"We're going to get those hats!" Billy yelled. "We're in first place!"

Michiko grimaced from the thumps her teammates gave her on the back.

The apple trees stood in fields of wheat-coloured summer grass dotted with lacy white flowers. School finished with the excitement of upcoming Dominion Day celebrations on July 1. There was to be a parade of servicemen, tug of war, sack races, and a huge game of bingo for the adults.

Michiko suggested to Tony that he strike a deal with her father. He could help with the farm work in exchange for lessons in woodworking. Sam and Tony made a good team both in the field and shed. But they both insisted on one thing. No one was to see what they were doing until the boxes were done, except for Mr. Takahashi, who was allowed to inspect at any time.

"We should do something special for Dominion Day," Michiko suggested to her mother.

"What do you have in mind?" her mother asked.

Michiko looked over at her little sister sleeping on the blanket in the shade. She remembered a picnic under a cherry tree, before they were forced to leave Vancouver, before Kaz met Sadie, before Hannah was born. "It's been a long, long time since we had a picnic."

Michiko's mother lowered the stick she was using to beat the rug on the clothesline. "We'll see," was all she said.

In the shade of a tree, Mr. Palumbo patted his breast pocket to find his pipe. He bent forward to shield the flame of his match from the breeze until the smoke escaped from the corner of his mouth. Then he settled on top of a turned-up crate to enjoy the day off. The two families had gathered to celebrate Dominion Day, but more importantly, the completion of Tony's woodworking project.

A wooden trestle table held the remnants of a summer feast. Michiko's contribution was a plate of the crispy marshmallow squares from Mary's party. To her surprise, the recipe was on the back of their new box of cereal, and using her berry money, she'd purchased a bag of marshmallows to surprise them all.

That wasn't the only surprise she planned to reveal. Her Uncle Kaz's latest letter waited in her blue box in her bedroom. It was short, but so important that Michiko decided it was time to share it with her parents.

Everyone admired Sam's small, polished maple chest. A tiny heart-shaped lock dangled from the front clasp. Her father stuck his hand in his pocket and pulled out a key attached to a length of string. "Little brothers are nosy," he said to her with a wink as he handed her the key.

Before Tony revealed the large box under the blanket, he cleared his throat and said, "After I show the box to the man in Toronto, it will be a gift for my mamma."

Mrs. Palumbo looked about and smiled. Michiko knew she didn't quite understand what was going on. She had seen that look on faces in the camp when English was spoken too fast.

He lifted the blanket with a flourish, and everyone gasped.

Rectangular in shape, with deep carvings on the front, it reminded Michiko of the kind of chest that carried treasure.

Sam pointed out the large dovetail corner joints and then raised the lid to reveal a second set of iron hinges inside.

Tony lifted out the fitted top tray and passed it to Mr. Palumbo for his approval.

Mr. Palumbo gripped the edge of the pipe in his teeth as he examined it.

Mrs. Palumbo ran her hands across the carvings with a grin.

"A very solid, well-crafted piece," Eiko said as she examined the box. "Good for you."

Back at the house, Michiko emptied her blue box and placed her grandfather's letters, tied with red ribbon, back inside. Then she set four packets of letters out on the kitchen table.

"You *have* been busy," her mother commented. "I thought you wrote to three soldiers."

"The fourth soldier is a very, very, very, special one," Michiko said as she pulled the thin blue paper from its envelope to read the last part of his most recent letter out loud. "When you hear it you will know why."

Congratulate me! I have been promoted to the rank of sergeant. You would think we would all be sent home now that the war is over, but we are needed now more than ever for what is called clean-up work. There is a chance I will get posted to Hong Kong as a member of the Canadian Intelligence Corps. Please keep in touch with your aunt. I know she will be lonely in Toronto.

Kaz

"You have been writing to Kaz?" her mother asked in surprise.

"All servicemen like mail," Michiko said. She paused for a moment and said, "It's really hard for them to be far away from their family and friends." She put the letter back into the envelope and placed it on top of his stack.

Her mother usually held back on her conversation until her father put down his chopsticks, but this time she spoke just as he filled his mouth. "You need to go with him."

"With who?"

"Antonio," she said, "when he shows his box to the furniture store owner."

"He doesn't need me, he's a big boy." Sam scowled and resumed eating.

"He will need help carrying it," Michiko said. "And your little box would fit inside."

Her father put his chopsticks down. "Leave Mr. Downey?"

"There will be plenty of men looking for work now that the war is over," Eiko said. She walked to him and placed her hand over his. "You gave up baseball for your family; don't give up woodworking. You know you love that more than planting bulbs."

Sam brushed her hand away, his eyes only half-rising from the table. Then he stood and headed for the door.

"Someone who stands behind a wall can see nothing else," Eiko said to his back.

But he did not respond.

That night, Tony knocked on Michiko's bedroom window. She wrapped her tiny *tansu* in a towel and passed it out to him.

The next morning, when Mr. Palumbo helped Tony

carry his treasure box to the Greyhound bus stop, Tony and Michiko exchanged a secret smile.

"So my dad says," Billy said, "why would I want to sell my farm? It's been in my family for generations." He wound up for a pitch and threw the battered baseball that the coach had given them toward Michiko. "Do you know what Mr. Leahey says?"

Michiko shook her head as she caught the ball.

Billy put his hands on his hips. "Leahey says my father will end up owning the only farm for miles, because everyone else is taking advantage of the war being over, selling up, and moving on with their lives." He caught the return ball, and the two of them took steps back.

"What did your dad say?"

Billy broke into a huge smile. "That's good, I'll have lots of business," but he didn't throw the ball as the two swerved their heads to see to who was coming down the lane.

A man in a brown uniform, with khaki puttees topping his highly polished boots, bicycled toward them in the middle of the afternoon. Under his large, peaked cap, a pencil stuck out from behind his ear. He leaned his bike against the maple tree and headed for Mr. Downey's front door. There he held out a flimsy yellow envelope. Michiko watched what happened next. She had seen the Western Union man deliver telegrams before, and it usually was bad news.

To her surprise, Mr. Downey stepped out and

accompanied the man to their front door. "Eiko?" he called out as the man waited at his side.

Michiko and Billy ran to see what was going on.

"It's a telegram," her mother said. "For your father."

"Who is it from?" Billy asked.

"Good news or bad, it will be shared after dinner," Eiko said, propping it up front of the sugar bowl.

Later, Michiko stood beside her father as he sliced the telegram open with a kitchen knife and read aloud.

Got job (stop)
Offer for my teacher too(stop)
Tony(stop)

Still holding the knife, Sam sank back into his chair. "I can't go till the end of the season."

"And I can't leave until the end of the baseball season," Michiko chimed in. She put her arm around her mother's waist. "I could stay and take care of Father. This time, you could go ahead and get everything settled."

Her mother rose from the table and picked up Hannah. "Surely Sadie would be able to find us a place in Toronto," she said.

"I don't even know where this place is," Sam muttered as he stuffed the telegram back into its envelope.

"I do," Michiko called out as she raced to her bedroom. She pulled the worn, folded advertisement from her little blue box. *Why didn't I notice that before?* she wondered. *The box is the same colour as Eddie's eyes.* She could use it for his letters when they moved to Toronto.

Author's Note

The names of the Japanese families are changed, but the people involved in Michiko's story are quite real. My mother-in-law, Eiko Kitagawa Maruno, allowed me to explore her life through personal photographs and memories. To better understand the family's experience in the internment camp of New Denver, my husband and I travelled through the Kootenay Mountains to the Nikkei Internment Memorial Centre.

Special thanks goes to Eiko's very good friend, Pat Adachi, whose father took her to all the Japanese baseball games, where she happily munched peanuts. Her published books, *Asahi Legends* and *The Road to the Pinnacle*, about the famed Asahi baseball teams, provided me with valuable information. These British Columbia teams are now honoured in the Canadian Baseball Hall of Fame.

The Canadian Army Language School opened in Vancouver, British Columbia, in August 1943. The

British Army needed men who could speak Japanese for service in Burma. Thirty-one Nisei swore allegiance to the King and enlisted in the Canadian Army. They were all sent to No. 20 Basic Infantry Training Camp at Brantford, Ontario. The Nisei were kept together as a platoon in B Company.

Early in 1945, Canada began to prepare a special force for the invasion of Japan, and Major Aiso visited the first Nisei group in basic training in Brantford to administer language tests to fifty-two recruits. From Brantford they went to Vancouver to attend the Canadian Army Japanese Language School. They were able to graduate from the twelve-month course in eight weeks, promoted to the rank of sergeant, and went overseas as members of the Canadian Intelligence Corps. By the time they reached the British Intelligence Corps in India, the war was over, but they were needed for clean-up work. Roy Ito's book, *We Went to War*, and the reports of Lt. W.H. Agnew, were valuable resources.

Pete Gray was not a publicity stunt. Named MVP in 1944, he batted .333, with 68 stolen bases.

The article about the All-American Girls Professional Baseball told the story of the Rockford Peaches, Fort Wayne Girls Club, South Bend Blue Sox, Kenosha Comets, Grand Rapids Chicks, Racine Belles, Anastasia Batikis, Annabelle Lee, Faye Dancer, Mary "Bonnie" Baker, and others. It appeared on page 63 of the sports section in *Life* magazine on June 4, 1945. I let Michiko read it two months earlier for the purpose of this novel; one bit of artistic license.

The Kellogg's Rice Krispies Marshmallow Treats recipe, first advertised in 1940, became a popular food for mailing to service people abroad.

It wasn't until January 2, 1945, that Canadian citizens of the Japanese race were freed from all federal or army supervision and allowed to go back to their homes. Having travelled so far from Vancouver, my husband's family did not consider returning, making Ontario their permanent home.

On September 22, 1988, Prime Minister Brian Mulroney attempted to right the wrongs of the internment with a formal apology and compensation for losses. His government also funded the Canadian Race Relations Foundation to ensure this would not happen again in our democratic country.

I am grateful to Sylvia McConnell for accepting my first manuscript, *When the Cherry Blossoms Fell,* which began The Cherry Blossom Series, and Allister Thompson with the editing process. Thanks also go to the team at Dundurn Press.

Sylvia McNicoll welcomed me to her writing group when I first moved to Burlington. Twice a month, Sylvia, Gisela Sherman, Amy Corbin, Claire Carver-Dias, Deborah Serravalle, Jim Bennett, Rory and Janice D'Eon, Chelsey Rainford, Steve Donnelly, and Sue Williams met. Thank you for running the bases with me.

To Stan, David, Erin, and Phil, I thank you for your never-ending support.

Glossary

Japanese vocabulary in order of appearance in the story

cha	tea
Yokohama	a large Japanese city
tokonoma	alcove for flower arrangements
origami	Japanese paper folding
hakujin	Caucasians or white people
sashimi	extremely sharp knife for slicing raw fish
yancha	naughty
Nisei	of the second generation
Issei	of the first generation
kaibutsu	monster
bok choy	Chinese cabbage
nappa	Japanese cabbage
tofu	bean cake
shoyu	soya sauce

miso	fermented bean paste
arigato	thank you
Itadakimasu	standard words given before a meal: I humbly receive
taiko	drumming
odori	dancing
Kamikaze	name given to suicide pilots in the Second World War
jidosha	car
yakyu	baseball
kami	god or divine spirit
kaze	breeze or wind
nori	toasted seaweed
chawanmushi	egg custard
yakitori	grilled on a skewer
kairanban	homemade newspaper or bulletin
hanten	housecoat
furoshiki	bundle made by tying four corners of a cloth square
tansu	hope chest
ronin	masterless warrior
shogun	general of/head of samurai government
mochi	Japanese rice cakes
itsu	when
gyoza	dumpling
okoko	odorous pickled vegetable root
gaman suru	be patient, put up with it
maho	magic

Italian vocabulary in order of appearance

buon giorno	good day, hello
si	yes
Signora	Mrs.
grazie	thank you
mi filio	my son
scarpe	shoes
Costa succedde?	What's happening?
Va!	Go!

Racial slang in order of appearance

Chink	a Chinese person
Eye-ties	Italians
Nips	Japanese (Nippon)

In the Same Series

When the Cherry Blossoms Fell

Short-listed for the 2012 Pacific Northwest Young Readers Choice Award and for the 2011 Hackmatack Children's Choice Award

Nine-year-old Michiko Minagawa bids her father good-bye before her birthday celebration. She doesn't know the government has ordered all Japanese-born men out of the province. Ten days later, her family joins hundreds of Japanese-Canadians on a train to the interior of British Columbia. Even though her aunt Sadie jokes about it, they have truly reached the "Land of No." There are no paved roads, no streetlights, and no streetcars. The house in which they are to live is dirty and drafty. At school Michiko learns the truth of her situation. She must face local prejudice, the worst winter in forty years and her first Christmas without her father.

Cherry Blossom Winter

Ten-year-old Michiko wants to be proud of her Japanese heritage but can't be.

After the bombing of Pearl Harbor, her family's possessions are confiscated and they are forced into deprivation in a small, insular community. The men are sent to work on the railway, so the women and children are left to make the trip on their own. After a former Asahi baseball star becomes her new teacher, life gets better. Baseball fever hits town, and when Michiko challenges the adults to a game with her class, the whole town turns out.

Then the government announces that they must move once again. But they can't think of relocating with a new baby coming, even with the offer of free passage to Japan. Michiko pretends to be her mother and writes to get a job for her father on a farm in Ontario. When he is accepted, they again pack their belongings and head to a new life in Ontario.